THE RIGHT TO BE

A Christopher Family Novel

W.D. Foster-Graham

authorHOUSE®

AuthorHouse™
1663 Liberty Drive
Bloomington, IN 47403
www.authorhouse.com
Phone: 833-262-8899

Published by AuthorHouse 04/06/2021

ISBN: 978-1-6655-2120-8 (sc)
ISBN: 978-1-6655-2119-2 (e)

Library of Congress Control Number: 2021906630

Print information available on the last page.

ACKNOWLEDGMENTS

I would like to acknowledge the following: Arthur and Shelly Foster; Patricia Knight; my fellow Sounds of Blackness alumni; my Central High classmates; my Luther College Black alumni; Kevin Moore; All God's Children MCC; my St. Peter's AME family; Rhonda Byrne, Lisa Nichols; LaTonia Williams; Frederick Smith; Terrance Dean; Cheryl Barton; Wyatt O'Brian Evans; Chase Connor; Blair Denholm; Kelvin Rodrigues; Evie Drae; James Earl Hardy; Queer in Color; Al McFarlane; DeWayne Davis; Jacki Renee; Georgina (Gigi) Kiersten; Jayce Ellis; Rayceen Pendarvis; my writer community on VSS365; Sharita Lira; Nhojj; Kevin E. Taylor; and to my Higher Power, who helped me find my authentic voice.

And to all my readers out there who believe in dreams and never give up. Representation matters.

This book is dedicated to Walter and to Edward Lee, and in memory of Dad, who encouraged me to be a storyteller.

AUTHOR'S NOTE

This is a work of fiction. Names, characters, places, and incidents either are the products of the author's imagination or are used fictitiously, and any resemblance to actual persons, living or dead, events, or locales is purely coincidental.

THE CHRISTOPHER FAMILY TREE

Allan Beckley Christopher (Maureen Moore)(married 1947)
- Martin Christopher (Terrence Williamson)(married 1975)
    - Crystal Christopher (Janice Taylor)(married 1988)
    - Martin Christopher, Jr. (Kareem Brown)(married 1988)
    - Dennis Christopher, II (Juniece Thompson)(married 1989)
    - Daphne Christopher (Tevin Marshall)(married 1998)
    - Valentine Christopher (Carlos Rivera)(married 1988)
    - Kelley Christopher (Rashid McNair)(married 1994)
- Joshua Christopher (Penelope Strand)(married 1969)
    - Ruby Christopher (Alejandro Perez)(married 1994)
    - Sadie Christopher (Sydney Browne)(married 2004)
    - Lorraine Christopher
    - Adele Christopher
- Marshall Christopher (Leroy Terrell)(married 1971)
- Katie Christopher (Raymond Sterling, Jr.)(married 1969)(Russell Johnson)(m. 1972)
    - Raymond Johnson (DeAndre Washington)(married 1990)
    - Harriet Johnson (Owen Boyd)(married 1997)
    - Alexander Johnson (Lakia Fuentes)(married 1996)
- Tanya Christopher (Teresa Johnson)(married 1973)
    - Tanisha Johnson-Christopher (Adrienne Boyd)(married 2000)
    - Imani Johnson-Christopher

Victoria Christopher (Travis Mitchell)(married 1996)
    Travis
    Traci
Allison Christopher (Michael Davis, Sr.)(married 1983)
    Michael Davis, Jr.
    Allan Davis
Bernard Christopher (Sherman Butterfield)(married 1988)
    Jesse
    Bruce
    Samuel

Chapter 1

December 31, 2005

The ocean breezes of a tropical evening caressed and cooled Allan Christopher Davis' body as he trudged along the road to his car, which was hidden by the foliage. He was reluctant to go home, at least so soon, and his identical twin brother Mickey had promised to give him a cover story about his whereabouts before he left the house. He reached the Range Rover in almost no time at all, sliding his muscular, 6'5" frame into it with ease. *New Year's Eve was OK, but it could have been much better.*

He let out a wistful sigh. No doubt Mickey had found a honey, and he was having a great time at one of the New Year's Eve parties in town. Not that he was jealous of his brother, he simply wanted that kind of fun for himself. Unfortunately, that wasn't the way things worked.

Lowering the windows and starting the vehicle, he headed up the road, with the wind blowing through his dreadlocks and no particular place to go. He found himself stopping at a deserted stretch of Viewpoint Beach. Maybe it was because his astrological sign was Pisces, but the water had always been a place where he could go, sit, and work things out in his mind. Although 2005 had been an active hurricane season that included Katrina, Rita, and Wilma, the Bahamas weren't as hard hit as other parts of the Caribbean and the U.S.; for that, he was grateful. He grabbed a beach towel, locking his car before he strolled down to the sand, ready for a skinny dip in the ocean.

The water soothed him, the gibbous moon in the sky reflected by the shimmering waves. Later, his body refreshed, Allan stretched out on his beach towel, his "Beckley eyes" drinking in the night scene before him, the calming sound of the water relaxing his mind… somewhat. He and his boyfriend, Thomas Hamilton, had had the same old argument an hour earlier before Allan left the no-tell motel in sheer frustration. They always had to meet in places way below the radar. Tonight, Thomas had been under him for nearly two hours and loved every minute of it, sharing passionate kisses and sweet nothings filled with desire and heat. However, he absolutely refused to be seen in public with Allan, much less entertain the notion of coming out. And Allan sincerely wanted a boyfriend who loved him, someone who wasn't afraid or ashamed to stand by him, the kind his cousins had.

Why, why did he have to get involved with a cop? That was one item on the laundry list of reasons Thomas gave him for keeping their relationship secret. Another one was Allan's age, since he was two months shy of his 18th birthday and Thomas was 25. Then there was Thomas' family and friends, his position in the community, and so on, and so on, and so on. After hearing them so often, they sounded more and more like excuses.

Topping the list was Allan's own lineage. He was the son of Michael and Lissa Davis of the internationally acclaimed jazz ensemble Sunrise, winners of multiple Grammys and numerous other music awards with enough gold and platinum records to give them legendary status in the music industry. He was named after his grandfather, self-made business mogul Allan Beckley Christopher, the founder of Christopher Electronics and the third African American billionaire in the U.S. His aunt, Victoria Christopher Mitchell, was the company's current CEO, and she made it a Fortune 100 company. Elijah Edwards, his first cousin twice removed, was an electronics whiz and instrumental in the expansion of the company back in the 1970s. Elijah's wife, Donna Gray Edwards—affectionately known in the family as Madear—was the queen of Twin Cities society, but she could easily reach across oceans to make things happen.

Although they retained their U.S. citizenship, his parents had made Nassau their home for many years. Having their level of fame, they said, was often a mixed blessing. Allan had been openly gay as long as he could remember, with the unconditional support of his family. No one on the islands dared to give him a hard time because of this celebrity status. Unfortunately, Thomas threw that fact in his face lately when they argued.

Not only did their status guarantee attention and stories but, like their parents, Allan and Mickey's looks never failed to turn heads. They had the sultry "Beckley eyes" they inherited from their grandfather, the aged ivory complexion, nose, and gap-toothed smile from their father, and the height from their mother. Sandy-brown dreadlocks reached to their waists, gracing bodies by Peterbilt with phat bubble butts supported by size 14 feet. In school, they led the pack as honors students. Their parents instilled in them from an early age that their looks were a gift and to treat them as such, but it didn't stop the overt female attention Mickey received and the covert male attention given to Allan.

During summer break mere months ago, Allan captured Thomas' attention. Thomas had attended a benefit concert given by Sunrise, all professional and police business—at first. The hot specimen of Bahamas' finest fell under the spell of Allan's "Beckley eyes" and subtly asked him out. One thing led to another, and a few dates later, Thomas was begging to be taken by Allan. The glow of passion and the desire to be together was good…to a point. The culture and environment surrounding them, however, was like a nimbus cloud tainted with fear, one that refused to go away.

Allan's eyes saddened as he lay there in solitude. He thought it would be different this time, different from the guys in his high school. Thomas may have been older than them, but he was still another in a line of boyfriends looking for monsters under the bed. Mom and Dad were concerned about his state of mind, as was Mickey. *Will things ever change here?* He'd made previous attempts in speaking up about the state of affairs for LGBTQ people on the islands along with the very few men and women who were out. Despite being born and raised in Nassau, his concerns were dismissed as those of an outsider. *I want what Mom and Dad have, but I'll never find that here. And if I leave, Thomas won't come with me.*

With the remnants of Thomas' scent washed off by the Atlantic and the reality of life in the Bahamas staring him in the face, a quote from an article he read online came to him: "If he won't come out, get out."

I have to get out, Allan said to himself, lifting his eyes toward the clear night sky as 2006 rolled in. *I can't stay here any longer...*

Chapter 2

January 2006

Allison Christopher Davis knew something was different about her son when he came downstairs the following morning. Allan, like Mickey, was outstanding in school and considered a well-adjusted 17-year-old, but he had been brooding for the past two months. She suspected his mood was connected to his mysterious boyfriend. She and her husband Michael had approached the subject with him on previous occasions only to get nowhere. Today, however, there was a look of resolution about him. *I wonder if it's related to our own decisions about this place.* Her musings were interrupted when Ms. Bond, their housekeeper, brought their Sunday breakfast to the dining room table.

Things were different when she and Michael moved there nearly 20 years ago after Sunrise broke onto the music scene with their now classic hits of "Afro Mystic" and "Indies Blues." She had fallen in love with the villa they made their home just outside of Nassau and the beauty of New Providence Island, not to mention Eleuthra, Bimini, and Grand Bahama; Sunrise had performed in all of the Bahama Islands and most of the Caribbean.

Their home and their lives were blessed with a double portion on February 29, 1988, when Michael Kennedy Davis, Jr. and Allan Christopher Davis were born 12 minutes apart, thanks to a history of multiple births on Lissa's side of the family. They weathered the joys and unique challenges of being in the entertainment industry on an international level of fame plus raising a family during their 22 years of marriage. The mere mention of the name Sunrise guaranteed sold-out concerts, like their last tour across the African continent and recent benefit concerts in Nassau and Freeport. However, the welcoming atmosphere of the islands back then was no longer as welcoming in her eyes now.

It had been fairly recent when the islanders showed inhospitality with a rather vocal protest against the LGBT family cruise hosted by Rosie O'Donnell, when the cruise liner came into port. For a nation whose primary industry was tourism, the incident made the islands look bad. She and Michael had shared many a conversation lately about their children's current situation, and they knew that matters had reached a crossroads. Mickey was regarded as a crown prince with all the bells and whistles, while Allan was merely tolerated because his parents' status protected him. Over time, Lissa realized that people may mutter things under their breath and gossip among themselves, but they wouldn't dare badmouth Allan in public, and her twins always had each other's backs. As for Michael and herself, their attitude was polite yet detached and guarded toward those islanders who weren't part of their inner circle.

While the family dined and the men engaged in small talk about the new year, Lissa's mind went back 18 years, when Michael had written the song, "The Right to Be." Their manager loved its reggae style, but he was strongly against producing the song because of the content. It was inspired by her younger brother Bernie's desire to take his Jamaican-born boyfriend Sherman to his high school prom in Evanston, Illinois. Many people considered it way ahead of its time, urging them not to do it. For Lissa and Michael, the decision was a no-brainer—they needed to look no further than their respective LGBTQ siblings, nieces, and nephews. Against all the odds, the song became a hit and won Sunrise their second Grammy award, after which they fired their manager. As for Bernie and Sherman, their dream manifested after Lissa's sister, Tanya Johnson-Christopher, filed a class-action lawsuit against the school district.

Right, right to be
Right, right to be
Who I am is who I am
I have the right to be...

The catchy refrain of the song stirred Lissa's spirits, yet she returned to the present upon hearing the words, "I can't stay here any longer."

"What do you mean, Allan?" Michael asked.

"It's this place. There's no future here for me."

"I think I know what you're getting at, but why don't you tell us?"

Her son took a deep breath and released it. "It's about the islands. They're beautiful, wonderful in many ways, but I don't feel equal here. I met this guy over summer break. I thought it would be different, but he's like all the others I dated. He refuses to even be seen in public with me, like he's terrified of his own shadow. Mickey can go anywhere around here, get a girl and everyone's OK with that. They're even cheering him on." Seeing the pain on his twin's face, Allan grabbed his hand. "I'm not saying that to dis you, Mickey. You've always had my back, and you've shut down anyone that tried to dis me or call me out.

The thing is, if I didn't have you and Mom and Dad, I'd be treated like a third-class citizen here. Oh, they don't come out and say things to my face, but I can sense the attitudes; I'm someone to be put up with. I know I can be a success in whatever career I choose, but I want what you have, too." Allan regarded his parents with wistfulness. "I want to marry the man I love someday, and I want kids. I don't see that happening here."

Silence prevailed for a minute while the family digested Allan's words. Finally, Mickey said, "If I can have a family, so should you. Nobody has the right to tell us we can't."

"Since this is a new year, now is the time to address this matter." Lissa looked at Michael, and he nodded. "Your father and I have also discussed this state of inequality here, and we've come to a decision."

"What?" Allan asked.

"After you two graduate from high school in a few months, we are closing up shop and moving back to the U.S."

Allan's eyes shifted from one parent to the other. "Are you sure?"

"Son, we've all felt it in the air. Sure, there will be plenty of people who will be unhappy about us pulling up stakes for various reasons. However, family comes first," Michael declared with calm finality.

"Sure. Besides, it's time for us to toughen up with some Midwestern winters," Mickey said jokingly. "And we'll be closer to Canada, so you can get married there."

The relief on Allan's face was music to Lissa's ears—and her heart. "Wow."

"To get your feet wet, so to speak, you two can visit your cousins in Minneapolis for spring break," Lissa added with a mischievous smile. "So buy whatever warm clothes you can find here for the trip. Whatever you can't get here, you can get there."

Though everyone was on board with the plans, Lissa noted Allan's expression switching to concern. "What about Ms. Bond and Mr. Garvey?" he asked.

"If they wish to come with us, we will do everything in our power to make that happen. If not, we will make sure they receive a generous severance package and excellent references when the time comes." Michael steepled his hands, a gesture Lissa knew indicated a done deal. "Right now, our plans will remain between us until it's closer to the time we leave."

When their sons left the dining room after breakfast, the change in Allan's walk was confirmation that they had made the right decision. A burden had been visibly lifted from his shoulders and tossed into the ocean. From the terrace balcony, they watched the twins engaging in horseplay as they took off down the road to the beach in celebration.

Michael put his arm around his beautiful, curvy, statuesque wife with a warm squeeze. The beauty on the inside of her only enhanced her outward appearance, her "Beckley eyes" and the wonderfully magnetic quality to her face framed by intricate braids, making her absolutely fabulous at 50. "Well, Lissa, it's done. We're on our way back to the U.S. Think Chicago is ready for us?"

"I don't know about Chicago, but Glen Ellyn has possibilities. The last time we were up there, I saw some lovely homes in the area."

"And these days, in those areas, the only color they're concerned about is the color of our money." Michael looked outside for a moment before he cast his eyes upon Lissa again. "You know, we have to let our parents know."

"Indeed, and make sure they know before anyone else tells them. This is the sort of news they don't need to hear from the media."

Later that day, Mickey and Allan relaxed by the lighthouse, watching the tourists come and go.

"It's going to be different, being back in the U.S.," Mickey said thoughtfully.

"You mean the whole celebrity thing?"

"Yeah. You remember what it was like, travelling with Mom and Dad around the world?"

Allan took a sip of bottled water. "Sort of. I thought all kids did that until we started kindergarten. Of course, here we're part of the scenery. Back in Chicago, people will probably look at us like they do Oprah."

"And we may wind up part of goodness knows how many stories, most of them made up. But you know Ms. Frazier won't stand for that."

Allan chuckled at the mention of Sunrise's agent, Okeidi Frazier. She had been with them since the group's early days, and the twins regarded her as an honorary aunt. "She'd tear them to shreds. What do you think she'll say about this?"

"Well...she's always respected Mom and Dad's wishes, but I think she'll be over the moon to have us back in Chicago." Mickey paused for a second to wave at some local girls before he turned back to his brother. "So, how's the new one coming?"

"Still needs work. If I change the lyrics in the second verse and slow down the tempo, I think it'll work better."

"Then you'll bring it to Dad?"

"I don't know yet. You know how Dad is."

Mickey rolled his eyes. "Yeah. Just like Grandpa when it comes to his craft. A perfectionist. He doesn't want just good. He wants *great.*"

"Well, at least he's only like that when it comes to the music." Allan scanned the clear blue Atlantic, feeling the breeze caressing his face before he spoke. "Remember the last time we went into town and split up, with you pretending to be me?"

A frown crossed Mickey's face. "I remember. They didn't say anything, but people were giving me these looks like they were judges and juries before I told them who I was. Then I let them have it."

"And I pretended to be you. The people I was around bragged about what a fine young man I was while they were trying to push their daughters on me. When I revealed myself, their smiles turned so fake."

"It used to be fun when we switched."

"Yeah. It drove the professors and the headmaster crazy."

"It's not fun anymore; not here. In any case, this will all be over soon. I'm sure a lot of people around here will be sorry for the way they treated you."

"That goes for you, too. A lot of those women aren't what they appear to be, and they'll be sorry for trying to use you. Anyway, now that we're leaving here, it's on to new adventures and something better. Ready for a swim?"

"Yeah. Let's enjoy this while we can," Mickey agreed as they rose and dashed off for the water.

A few hours later, Michael emerged from the studio to find his wife seated in the family room, phone in hand.

"Who are you calling, honey?"

“Mother and Father. We agreed they need to be informed of our plans, and there’s no time like the present. After that, I’m calling Wayne and Theo. We can’t just spring the twins on them without advance notice.”

Michael ran a hand lazily through his long, sandy brown dreadlocks, now graced with strands of grey. “True. I’m assuming they can be trusted to keep things under wraps.”

“Of course they can. Remember Father’s 60th birthday party?”

“How can I forget it?” he chuckled. “The family was better at keeping *that* secret than the CIA ever could.”

“And in our family, we know the main ones to avoid. Cousin Brenda and Cousin Bertha.” Lissa shuddered at the thought of their arrival being prematurely plastered on every news and print media outlet in the U.S. because of her gossipy, blabbermouth cousins. Regaining her composure, she asked, “When are you going to tell the band?”

A fond smile spread across Michael’s face. Having an ensemble of original members that was still together after 30-plus years was rare in the industry, and he looked upon Ronnell Hayes, Sol Harvey, Jalani Austin, and Medford Gladstone as brothers. Sure, they had their share of rocky times, as every group does, but they had paid their dues and gotten through. “Not yet, but soon. I think it’s best we keep this limited to immediate family for now. The good thing is, they’re all still in the Chicago metro area. But I will tell my mother when you’re done.”

“OK. You know we also have to tell Okeidi.”

“Yes, she’s on the short list.”

“Now, what about Glenn? Won’t that be tricky, with him having Jeffrey as a husband?”

Given the reminder of his brother being married to, of all people, Cousin Bertha’s son, Michael grew pensive. “Wellllll…I could swear Ma to secrecy on this news. Glenn is a bad liar. Jeffrey only has to look at his face, and he’ll pick up on it. After that, all bets are off.”

“Then it’s settled. We tell our parents, Cousin Wayne, and Okeidi first.”

Relaxing in his king-sized bed that night, Mickey slipped a Bob Marley disc into his CD player. It was a legacy from his infant days, something his father came up with in a burst of inspiration, and he knew he'd fall asleep in about half an hour. It did create a minor problem for his parents on the occasions when the family attended a Marley family concert, as did the snoring trait common among Davis men. Still, it was what it was.

Hearing what his twin shared with him when they switched identities bothered Mickey more than he thought. It wasn't only because of the way Allan was treated but because of the number of young ladies—and their parents—seeing him as a meal ticket to a huge gravy train. Sure, he had been sexually active given the age of consent on the islands was 16, but he was no fool. No matter how much a girl begged to feel him "skin to skin" inside her, Mickey always wore a condom with the few partners he had slept with. As added insurance, he kept the condom with him at all times and put it on himself. Dad had warned him about women who put holes in condoms in order to deliberately get pregnant; Mom referred to them as "scheming tarts."

He was realistic enough to know there were probably women like that back in the U.S. Like Allan, he wanted to make something of himself. One day, he would find the right woman, one with goals of her own and who could handle having a husband in the music industry—as well as his snoring. *One day, I'll be part of Sunrise.*

Slowly, he drifted off to sleep. *Wouldn't it be a mindblower if we met up with twins? Brother-sister twins. I'd have a wife, and Allan would have a husband. Sometime in the future...*

Long after Mickey went off to his room, Allan lay awake in bed, staring out the window at the ocean after changing the lyrics to his song. *It isn't a dream. We're really going back.* The sigh he breathed was fraught with anticipation. It had been two years since the last major Christopher family reunion, when all the branches of the family came together in Kansas City, Missouri. The Devereaux branch came up from Atlanta, Great-great-uncle Josiah Christopher's branch flew in from Rockford and Milwaukee, the Edwards branch came down from Minneapolis, and their branch came over from greater Chicago back then. For their upcoming spring break trip, Mom said he and Mickey would be staying with Cousin Wayne, his husband Theo, and their sons, who were close to his age.

His great-uncle Sammy, at 84, was considered the gay elder of the family. Allan had been an infant at the time, but his parents, aunts, and uncles had told him the story surrounding his grandfather's 60th birthday and their efforts to reunite Sammy with his brother. It had backfired initially, but family secrets were revealed that ultimately resolved matters between his grandfather and Uncle Sammy. At the reunion, Allan asked Sammy and his current partner, Darnell Smith, "So when are you two gonna tie the knot?" The fact that Uncle Sammy had been with his previous partner for 41 years made the question a valid one, and he and Darnell had been together nine years at that point. His 17-year-old mind told him his great-uncle deserved to make his love match permanent, with marriage equality being on the table in Canada. Besides, with rare exceptions, longevity in relationships was a Christopher family trait.

On an impulse, Allan picked up his phone and dialed. Uncle Sammy's birthday was coming up the day after tomorrow, and with the latest happenings in his family, Allan considered it a most opportune time to call him. Besides, with the three-hour time difference, he should still be up.

"Hey, Uncle Sammy. It's Allan…"

Chapter 3

January 2006

Sammy Christopher finished a leisurely cup of coffee and adjusted his Stetson to protect his eyes from the California sun, sitting in his rocking chair on the porch of his home. It overlooked the 300 acres of his ranch in San Bernardino County, the largest county by area in California and the continental U.S. This was the ranch where he and John Lee Burton put down roots and built a life together over 50 years ago. His veterinary skills, combined with John Lee's knowledge and ability with horses, had made their business lucrative for decades. They were highly respected in the area, the go-to couple when it came to horse breeding. And now the time had come for him to make and finalize decisions about the future of the ranch.

He rocked with a slow but steady pace, memories of the business and John Lee floating through his mind like the cirrus clouds in the sky. It had been 18 years since his first life partner passed away, yet a part of him still lived on. Where did the years go? Sammy's birthday—January 3—seemed to come around faster with each passing year, but that was far better than the alternative. He and Darnell had spent it with his large extended family in Chicago, where he maintained a sumptuous condominium on North Marine Drive. Staying active on the ranch and networking with friends and family had kept him quite spry for a man of 85, something his brothers—Dennis, Amos, and Allan—didn't hesitate to comment on. The one somber note on the occasion was his brother Franklin's absence, given his passing three months earlier.

His niece, Tanya Johnson-Christopher, was a prominent civil liberties attorney in Chicago, and she and her wife Teresa had taken him aside during the festivities to give him a gentle but loving reminder about making sure all his affairs were in order. In the past, he put it off. Now, with more years behind him than ahead of him, that was no longer an option. He wanted to ensure the ranch and the horses were placed in hands that would love them as much as he did. Not only that, Darnell agreed with Tanya

When he and Darnell Smith first met in 1994, they found themselves sharing the common bond of being World War II veterans and widowers from long-term relationships. In addition, at one time, Darnell was the boyfriend of Sammy's cousin from Atlanta, Bernard Devereaux, Jr. Junior, as he was called by his family, had died in Germany in 1945 when he stepped on a mortar. Sadly, his death was witnessed by Darnell. After the war, Darnell chose to live in Paris, where some years later he met Rene' Charlevoix, a Haitian living in the city and the man he would spend 36 years of his life with until his death in 1987. Shameless matchmaking on the part of his younger cousins in Atlanta brought the two together, and now, 11 years later, Sammy was glad they did.

As chief beneficiary in his current will, Darnell would inherit the ranch and the business, in order to pass the torch to someone younger. Sammy wanted to keep the ranch in the family, and at present, the best candidate was his wisecracking nephew Bernie, who was well respected as Bernard Christopher, DVM, a sought-after veterinarian. His husband, Sherman, a Jamaican turned U.S. citizen, had a lucrative practice as an attorney. They were raising three sons, something that wasn't even thought of when Sammy was a young man unless it was under the radar. The question was, would they consider relocating to California?

Sammy smiled as he thought of his position in the family as the gay elder. With so many LGBTQ nephews, nieces, grandnephews, and grandnieces, not to mention cousins in the extended Christopher family, it was normal to hear from any one of them at least two or three times a week, seeking advice or just wanting to talk. The most recent one to call was his grandnephew, Allan Davis. Last night, Allan had been down in the dumps about his boyfriend troubles and his present situation in the Bahamas, needing to vent. Sammy had listened quietly, sharing his own experiences as a young gay man when asked.

"There's something else I wanted to tell you, Uncle Sammy." The tone of Allan's voice indicated a juicy secret was about to be divulged.

"Oh? And what's that?"

"We're all moving back to Illinois."

The happiness in Sammy's voice broke free. "You are? When?"

"Right after Mickey and I graduate."

"That's great! Fabulous news! I can understand some of the fear in that environment, but you still deserve far more than what you're getting. I have no doubt that there are plenty of eligible men here in this country for you."

"I hope so," Allan sighed. "Mom and Dad want to wait until a couple of weeks before we move to go public with it. Are you and Uncle Darnell going to come visit after we get back?"

"We're only a plane ride away, Allan. One of the advantages of retirement," Sammy said, chuckling. "Just say the word, and we're there. What did Okeidi say when you told her?"

"Are you kidding? When Dad told her what we planned, she was over the moon. Of course, she totally appreciates why everything is under wraps for now, but I know she'll waste no time lining up concerts and press conferences as soon as Mom and Dad say the word."

"In other words, the powers that be over there will see a revenue and publicity source vanish when you leave, and they won't be happy about that. And then there's your closet case cop that wants to drag you into the closet with him."

"Yeah," Allan admitted.

"Any chance of that situation changing? Maybe he'll realize his mistake and leave the islands to be with you?"

"No, Uncle Sammy. Thomas is a lost cause, and I've had to accept that."

"Well, it's his loss. You, on the other hand, have a whole new world waiting for you. Have you thought about where you want to go for college?"

"Mickey and I are going to visit Cousin Wayne and his family up in Minneapolis during spring break. Maybe I'll go to school there."

"From what I know, the Twin Cities have plenty of good colleges and universities going for it. It wouldn't hurt to check it out. So, how's Mickey?"

"Cool as ever. Always the ladies' man, but definitely no fool."

"How do you mean?"

Allan paused for a moment. "It hasn't been easy for him, either. I mean, who wants to be thought of as a lottery ticket? He's had girls after him, wanting him so they can get their hands on our money and cash in on the Sunrise fame. If not the girls themselves, it's their relatives that are pushing them."

"I get it, Allan. The road to love is more complicated when you're in the public eye. I have to say, Lissa and Michael raised you right. Both of you deserve the best, people who truly love you. You may not believe me now, but when the right one comes along, you'll know it. And there's no rush. You're young. You have plenty of time ahead of you."

"OK, Uncle Sammy. I'm going to let you go. And tell Uncle Darnell I said hi."

"I will. Bye."

Sammy's laugh lines appeared upon the memory of the call. *No one is going to push Little Allan around.* He was certain that a number of people on the islands would be eating their words for breakfast when the Davis family pulled up stakes for good. And once his brother got wind of the news, he would move Mt. Everest to help them return if they ever needed it. If necessary, Allan Beckley Christopher would reach across the water and deal swiftly with anyone who hurt his grandsons. He had truly come a long, long way from the brother who had disowned him nearly 60 years ago, which turned out to be guilt over a fire that caused the burns Sammy bore on his back and arms today.

Mickey and Little Allan were barely three months old during that fateful May of 1988. Encouraged by a surprise visit from Allan's children, the nephews and nieces he had never met, Sammy had agreed to be part of the 60th birthday festivities for his brother, which included a stage show. The surprise reunion had backfired, but it unknowingly served as the catalyst which stirred up haunting memories Allan had repressed for 48 years. That event, combined with John Lee's death shortly afterwards, ultimately led to a reconciliation between the two brothers.

Over the years, the Christopher family had experienced its share of the successes and challenges of life, but they steadily grew closer. The older members of the family, like himself, preferred to keep in contact through phone calls and letters, while the younger ones used the modern technology of electronic mail and text messaging. His sister-in-law, Dr. Maureen Moore Christopher, along with his cousin, Deborah Edwards Hendricks, had taken on the mantle of family historians. He had been happy to contribute photographs of himself and John Lee back in the day as well as other memorabilia of the years that followed. To further their legacy, his generation continued grooming the succeeding generations to assume their place in the family businesses as well as the family.

From his phone call with Little Allan, it was no surprise to Sammy to learn that Mickey inherited his father's musical ability while Little Allan turned out to be a songwriter. When last he heard from Mickey, it was apparent he had his heart set on becoming part of Sunrise; all he had to do was learn to live with his father's high standards. Sammy hoped Michael wouldn't make the same mistakes that Allan had. When his son Josh wanted to come into Christopher Electronics decades ago, Allan took his perfectionistic tendencies too far and drove Josh into quitting the company. He was disappointed when none of his other sons wanted to go into the company, but he ultimately learned from his mistakes when his daughter Vickie showed an interest in the business. In turn, she made it even better and more successful once appointed CEO.

Sammy's reminiscing was interrupted by his housekeeper, Iris, holding a cordless phone in her hand. "Mr. Christopher, it's for you. Your brother."

"Which one?"

"Allan."

"Thanks, Iris." Sammy accepted the phone. "Hey."

"Hey, Sammy, what's going on."

"Beckley," he said with a smile in his voice, using the name he had called his younger brother since childhood. "It's good to hear your voice. I'm just relaxing on the porch. My foreman is checking on the mares. Half of them are pregnant, so we'll be busy when foaling season comes."

"Business is booming, I take it."

"It sure is, but I know it's time for me to pass the torch."

"Any candidates in mind?"

"I've thought of a few. The main thing is, I want to keep the business in the family. What's going on with you?"

"Sammy, I just received the greatest news. Allison and Michael and the boys are coming back—for good!"

The excitement in his brother's voice warmed Sammy's heart. "That's great, Beckley. When are they coming?"

"As soon as the twins graduate. And if anyone over there interferes, I will personally make their lives miserable," Allan vowed.

"I know that's right. I feel the same way. But I'm sure Lissa and Michael have the situation well in hand, and they know they can come to you if they need to."

"True. In any case, they deserve a welcome-home celebration. I know I can count on you and Darnell to be there."

"Of course. Give us a date and the reservations will be booked."

"How about if Vickie sends the jet out there to pick you up?"

"That's even better."

"Great. How's Darnell?"

"His arthritis kicks up every now and then, but otherwise he's good."

"Isn't it something, the way our conversations change over time? When we were younger, it was all about how we were going to take the world by the tail."

"And now it's about health, retirement, grandchildren," Sammy laughed.

"Do you regret it, though? Not having children?"

Sammy was quiet for a moment. "If the times had been different back then, Beckley, I think John Lee and I would have made great parents. Fortunately, that desire is now filled with the grands and the great-grands in nieces and nephews. And of course, I have Darnell, my second chance at love."

"And you more than deserve it, Sammy. Now, given certain people in the family—and we know who they are—I have promised to keep the good news under tight security until Allison and Michael announce it, which will be closer to the time they leave."

"I hear you. So, they already have a plan in place?"

"They do, and I'm sure they'll be successful in carrying it out."

Sammy and Allan continued to discuss family and business for a while before the conversation ended. Setting the cordless phone down on the little serving table, Sammy took a moment to clean his bifocals, then stood up and stretched. He walked down the front steps from the porch, heading leisurely to the pasture where one of their prize stallions, Mister Magic, was being put through his paces by his foreman Benjamin, Iris' husband. His knowledge of horses and blood lines had translated into handsome stud fees for Mister Magic, and with the help of Darnell and his team at the ranch, business continued to prosper.

Engrossed in watching Mister Magic, he almost didn't notice the hand on his shoulder. "Hey, honey. How did it go in town?" he beamed.

Darnell looked down at his partner, the laugh lines on his deep brown face crinkling with success. "Great. Our new clients have been vetted, and the paperwork is being processed."

Sammy wrapped Darnell in his arms, giving him a warm kiss. "I'm glad. I was thinking about the practice and the ranch, too."

"As far as?"

"Grooming a successor."

"I take it you have someone in mind."

"Yeah. I was thinking of Bernie and Sherman."

Darnell nodded. "I have to say they have all the credentials to run it. Plus, it would keep everything in the family. I know that's important to you."

"And this would be a great place for their kids. I just hope they can see moving out here."

"Well, since they grew up in Chicago, perhaps having L.A. only an hour away would be a perk," Darnell suggested and then quipped, "when traffic is good."

Sammy gave a little laugh. "In that case, let's go for it and hope for a yes. By the way, I talked to Beckley before you got here."

"How is he?"

"Thrilled," Sammy beamed. "Lissa and Michael's family is moving back to Chicago."

"Moving? That's huge."

"It is. Little Allan told me about it the other day."

"So why am I only hearing about this now?"

"Because he swore me to secrecy. A big part of the reason they're moving back is because of the way he's been treated over there." Sammy's eyes narrowed for a moment.

Darnell's lips set in a grim line before he spoke. "When will that bullshit ever end?"

"Well, I'd say we still have a long way to go, even though we've come a long way. The good thing is, with his parents being such big names in the music industry, having that kind of support is going to go far. And they're not afraid to speak out." Sammy took Darnell's hand. "I don't know about you, but I'm hungry. What say we see what Iris has cooked up?"

"Sounds like a plan."

That night, after Darnell feel asleep while spooning him, Sammy was sated and happy. They made love on a lesser frequency than they did when they were young men, but the quality of their lovemaking more than made up for that. He loved the way he felt when Darnell was inside him, as he had been just an hour or so earlier. Darnell, on the other hand, bottomed occasionally, but when he did, it was still hot.

Being part of the day-to-day operations of running a ranch kept the couple both active and in good shape, one of the benefits being their ongoing love life. His great-grandnephews and great-grandnieces scoffed at first at the idea of him and Darnell being sexually active, to which he replied, "Just because there's snow on this roof, doesn't mean there's no fire in the furnace."

It also makes a huge difference when it's someone you love, and I love this man. While he listened to the crickets chirping in the night, be basked in his fondness and love for Darnell Brian Smith. *He's tough when he needs to be, he has this laugh-out-loud sense of humor, and the romantic in him...all those years he lived in Paris certainly paid off there. When the going gets tough, Darnell is a rock. He is, without a doubt, a ride-or-die guy. I hope Little Allan finds that kind of love. A ride-or-die guy.*

As Sammy snuggled deeper into Darnell's embrace and the haze of slumber approached, thoughts of what his younger relatives had learned from him, and vice versa, played on his mind. *It's time I made that call...*

Chapter 4

Spring 2006

Ms. Bond outdid herself with the three-tiered cake she baked for Mickey and Allan's 18th birthday. True, February 29 was their actual birthday, but they had no problem celebrating it on the 28th. It would have been easy for them to go out to a club and dance the night away, given the occasion. Instead, they chose to spend a laid-back birthday at home among the few close friends they had, their parents, Ms. Bond, and Mr. Garvey.

Birthday wishes poured in from family as well as Sunrise fan mail. Knowing they'd never get through all the fan mail, the twins asked for Okeidi's help in handling it. Relatives were contacted directly, via Skype, email, and phone.

"All right, sons, you know the drill. Make your wishes, blow out your candles," Michael stated.

"Tell you what. I'll take one side, you take the other," Allan offered.

"Deal." Mickey faced off his twin on the other side of the table.

Between the two of them, they managed to blow out the candles—all but one. After some unsuccessful attempts to do so, they happened to look up and catch the smirk on Michael's face; they'd been had.

"Good one, Dad, good one." Allan tried for deadpan sarcastic, but he could only suppress a laugh for about three seconds, which triggered laughter from the group.

"So, what did you wish for?" Lissa asked them.

"Mom, you know it's bad luck to tell," Mickey answered as he took a huge slice.

"Right," Allan concurred, sitting down to a considerable slice of his own. *Besides, I bet you already know. Three more months, and we're out of here.*

Of all the spring breaks they'd experienced, this was the first one that had Allan shopping for clothes to put on rather than take off—unless they wanted to take their chances with hypothermia and frostbite on Minneapolis' lakes in early April, according to his cousin, Wayne Hendricks-Bell.

"Honey, the worst of the winter has already passed, so you're getting off easy this time," Cousin Wayne said during one of their phone calls prior to departure. "Besides, Ronnell and Jermaine can hardly wait to see you."

"Ronnell? You know that's the name of our keyboard player in Sunrise."

"We know that, Allan. Your cousin Theo and his brother Brian are huge Sunrise fans, and Theo insisted that we name our older son after him."

"I'm sure our Ronnell will be very honored to hear that, if he doesn't already know."

"Do you think Sunrise will come to Minneapolis sometime in the future?"

Allan snickered. "Well, I'd like to think I have some pull with at least two of the members."

"Honey, if you do, you know who'll be buying front row seats."

Allan ended the call laughing to himself, wondering if they knew that Ronnell had more in common with his namesake than a first name. If they were that big as fans, they probably did. From sitting in on rehearsals while Mickey was practicing on his bass, he had picked up on certain looks that passed between keyboardist Ronnell Hayes and Jalani Austin, Sunrise's drummer. He may have been 15 at the time, but he knew what those looks meant. When Ronnell and Jalani later announced they were a couple, the response from the respective ensemble was, "Cool. We were wondering what took you so long," and went on without missing a beat. All in all, it was always good to see another mature Black male couple going strong.

At Nassau International Airport five weeks later, Lissa and Michael embraced their sons. "Now, make sure you call us at the layover and as soon as you get to Minneapolis," Lissa urged.

"We will, Mom," was Mickey's reply.

"Promise?"

Mom, you're hovering. Of course, the twins wisely kept this to themselves and answered instead, "Promise."

The flight, including layover, took about a day. Being who they were, Allan and Mickey were grateful for the first-class seats that provided the necessary room for their 6'5", 250 lb. frames. When they weren't watching the in-flight movies, Mickey brought music while Allan had reading material. His favorite authors were his cousin, John Gray Edwards—a renowned author of action/intrigue novels—plus Brenda Jackson and Sylvia Berry Lewis, who spun masterful tales of family and romance.

Leaving the customs area of the Hubert H. Humphrey international terminal in Bloomington, Minnesota, they were greeted with warm and hearty hugs from Cousin Wayne, his husband Theo, and their sons. Once again, Allan was reminded of how height ran in the family, with Wayne standing at 6'6", Theo at 6'2", and Ronnell at 6'2". Well, all except Jermaine, who was 5'11", but it was still respectable.

"Honey hush, you finally made it here," Cousin Wayne beamed. "Now, let's get your bags and get you out of here before you attract too much attention."

"And hope we don't run into a Sunrise welcoming party," Cousin Theo added. "You'll get enough of that from Brian."

When they stepped outside the terminal to the parking ramp, Allan was glad they had listened to their mother and wore sweaters and coats. By Minneapolis standards of early spring, the temperature was a reasonable 49 degrees, but to them, after years of life in a tropical climate, the weather was on the cold side. Sure, their parents had brought them to visit Chicago periodically, but it was always during late spring, summer, and very early fall. Minneapolis was a different animal altogether. Noting the way his cousin's arms were wrapped around himself, Jermaine commented, "It doesn't seem like it, Allan, but it gets better. Just give it time."

"How much time?" Allan wondered.

"When summer gets here—and it will—you'll feel it."

"Besides, Minnesota is all about outdoor activities. From what I see, I think you'll like that," Ronnell added after giving the twins the onceover.

The drive from the airport to Cousin Wayne and Cousin Theo's home on Lake Nokomis was relatively quick, given the flight's early afternoon arrival. Allan was intrigued by Minneapolis' distinctive lake and parkway system as his cousins gave him and Mickey more pointers about the Twin Cities area. When they arrived and settled in, Cousin Wayne prepared a late lunch, the kind that "sticks to your ribs."

"How long have you and Cousin Theo been together now?" Allan asked as they ate.

Wayne gave Allan a fat smile. "Honey, we're 30 years in, and it's been worth every year."

Allan reflected on the long-term relationships of his uncles and aunts for a moment and smiled in return. "Cool. Now, for the big question. How did the two of you meet?"

Cousin Theo, who could have been an older version of Jensen Atwood, squeezed Wayne's hand. "We met in the dead of summer at a Sounds of Blackness concert. Wayne here is their Number One camp follower, next to my brother Brian. Any mention of a Sounds gig around here, and he's there. Plus, he's made sure we never miss their Christmas program. He was sitting with your cousins, Junior and Sandra. Our eyes met, and that was that."

"And let's not forget the next evening," Cousin Wayne teased. "That was when we went to see *Jaws.*"

"One of my lesser moments," Cousin Theo conceded. "But we've been together ever since."

"We'd never see anything like that in Nassau, at least not out in the open," Mickey stated. "But we won't be there much longer. Frankly, I'm glad."

"Counting down the days, huh?" Ronnell asked.

"You know it. Between the dudes who wimp out on Allan and the women who want a baby on me like a winning lottery ticket, enough is enough."

Jermaine shook his head. "Hopefully, you'll have better prospects here. Minnesota's supposed to be a good place for couples and families. Just look at Dad and Pops."

"Not to mention most of your Edwards Cuznet." Wayne washed down a bite of cornbread with soda. "Now, your Cousin Mel and your Cousin Douglass may not be there yet, but trust and believe, they will be. Take it from Mother Wayne, it's only a matter of time." Wayne snapped his fingers for emphasis.

Later that evening, the cousins gathered in Jermaine's room, listening to Destiny's Child and Beyonce. They sang and danced to Beyonce and Jay-Z's "Crazy in Love" video, engaging in friendly competition for who could do the best twerk.

"Now, what's the night life like here?" Allan asked after the video ended.

"Most of the clubs are downtown, either on Hennepin or First Avenue North," Ronnell answered. "Thing is, you have to be 21 to get in most places, unless you look it. Then again, if you're hanging with an older crowd, you may not be looked at too closely. There is one place we can go on Hennepin, only because it's a juice bar. Downtown pretty much closes up at one a.m., but if you're in the network, you can usually find a party on weekends. And of course, you have lots of cousins here to hang out with."

"Good to know when we need a break from studies. What about college?"

"Lots of them around here, but I can only speak for the U of M. That's the biggest one. It's so big that it sits on both sides of the river and has its own downtown area. We call it Dinkytown."

Mickey smirked. "Let me guess. You go there, don't you?"

"Guilty as charged." Ronnell blew on his glitter nails. "I'm a fierce sophomore."

"And Pops is a professor there," Jermaine threw in. "He can put in a good word for you if you want to go. But he'll only do it if your grades are good."

The twins exchanged a thoughtful look before Allan spoke. "Do you think he could set up a tour?"

"The admissions office opens on Monday. We can ask him."

On Saturday evening, Allan and Mickey's Edwards relatives threw a party at Cousin Eli and Madear's mansion on Lake of the Isles Parkway, formally welcoming them to Minneapolis. Three years had passed since they last saw them, and it was great to be embraced by the warm hospitality. For Allan, having extended family here plus LGBTQ relatives felt like a lush oasis after spending years in the Kalahari Desert—at least, that was what the past year was like.

It was a kick to see his older relatives, like Cousin Wayne, Cousin Julian, Cousin Doris, and Cousin Douglass, partying with their spouses to the old-school jams like Gloria Gaynor's "Anybody Wanna Party," Donna Summer's "Hot Stuff," Patrice Rushen's "Hang It Up," and Kool and the Gang's "Funky Stuff." As he and his twin engaged in the various conversations that reconnected them between times on the dance floor, Allan found himself wishing again that graduation could be over and done with—like yesterday. *This is what life could be like.*

On Sunday morning, the twins were up and out of the house with their cousins for church—early morning service at St. Matthew's AME Church and mid-morning service at Light of the World Tabernacle. The fact that their cousin, Darrell Edwards, was an associate pastor at Light of the World, was encouraging, not to mention the way Darrell's wife and children were embraced by the predominately LGBTQ congregation of color.

Late Monday morning found Allan, Mickey, and Cousin Theo at the admissions office in Williamson Hall, ready for a tour. Satisfied with the results of a phone call with their parents over the weekend, Theo Hendricks-Bell was happy to use whatever influence he possessed to get them accepted should they choose to attend the U of M.

"That campus is huge," Allan sighed afterward, when he and his brother sat down for lunch at McDonald's on Southeast Fourth Street in the heart of Dinkytown.

"We'll need a map to get around there, at least for a while." Mickey took a sip of his Sprite. "With that many students, it should be easy to blend in and get our degrees with no sweat."

"Unless you decide to get on any of the Gophers teams."

"Me? What about you?"

Allan finished nibbling on a French fry. "You know I only like to play B-ball for fun. Otherwise, I'm like Cousin Wayne."

"In any case, with Sunrise based in Chicago, who would even think to look for us here? The best thing is, we already have family up here."

"It's something to seriously think about. Anyway, there's that matter of getting our school transcripts sent to whatever college we choose without tipping our hand." He took a moment to savor his quarter-pounder, viewing the sheer numbers of students walking about the area outside. "Scratch that. Mom and Dad will find a way."

"And Grandpa Allan, Grandma Maureen, and Grandma Saralynne will serve as backup. In the meantime, let's check out downtown. You know what Dad said before we left: 'Learn your way around the place.'"

After dropping in on Cousin Wayne at his office in the Hennepin County Government Center, navigating downtown Minneapolis' extensive skyway system, and shopping along the Nicollet Mall, the twins were ready to relax back at their cousins' home.

"What do you think about coming here?" Mickey kicked off his Nikes and stretched out on a bed.

Allan followed suit on the other bed. "It sounds like a plan. The Twin Cities is close enough to get to Chicago but far enough away where the media won't think of looking for us."

Mickey cracked his knuckles, locking his hands behind his head. "And the big thing is, we have family around us who have our backs."

"Yeah. Everyone but Cousin Xenobia."

"I know." Mickey frowned at the memory of her attitude at the party. Xenobia, looking down her nose at the twins, had dismissed them as 'common ruffians.' "She's a total bitch on wheels. Nobody likes her. But Cousin Wayne put in a word to Madear and his mom, so she shouldn't give us any trouble."

"I hope not. Anyway, aren't we supposed to meet some more family tomorrow?"

"Yeah. Cousin Theo's side. They live out in Robbinsdale."

To Allan's delight, the Bell family gathered together and greeted them with open arms. Of Carl and Melanie Bell's five sons, 18 grandchildren, and a growing number of great-grands, he could count the number of girls in the family on one hand. However, his gaydar immediately zoomed in on several of Cousin Theo's nephews, even before Ronnell and Jermaine mixed and mingled. *Does it get any better than this?*

Brian, the oldest of Cousin Theo's brothers, gave them friendly brotha hugs, after which he stood back and scrutinized the twins. "You two…there's something about you two that's very familiar."

"Oh?" Mickey asked casually.

"Yeah. It's just that I can't…" His jaw dropped to the floor. "I knew it. *I knew it!!!"*

"Knew what?"

"Don't try and play me, Mickey. Your parents are part of Sunrise. I can see how much you two favor them!" Brian was drooling at the prospect of receiving inside information about his favorite group.

"Hold on, hold on, back it up a little," Cousin Wayne admonished his brother-in-law. "Before you go off and tell everyone in the Twin Cities, they're here because they *don't* want attention from the media. They want to attend school in peace."

Brian's expression was a mixture of unbridled enthusiasm and frustration until Cousin Theo followed up with, "Brian, let's do it like this. I'm sure Allan and Mickey can tell you certain things about their lives and the ensemble that the public doesn't know. But outside of family, it's important for now that you keep it to yourself. Just know that you'll always have inside information that others don't. That ought to be worth some satisfaction."

"Well…all right. But you're not leaving here 'til you tell me more about life down there," Brian conceded.

"We promise," Allan said.

"But don't you monopolize all their time, Brian," Mrs. Bell warned. "Now that that's settled, these young men need to be fed."

From the spread laid out before them, the twins recognized Melanie Bell as part of that generation of Black women who loved to see their men eat; the more they ate, the greater the compliments she received. By the time the group finally left and headed back to Minneapolis, Allan and Mickey were in a blissful food coma. Ronnell, his boyfriend Lamar King, and Jermaine were in a similar condition.

"Man, between Mrs. Bell, your dads and all, one thing we'll never do here is starve." Mickey collapsed into a comfortable chair in the family room.

"Not as long as you're in this house." Jermaine patted his full stomach in confirmation. "And while you're here, Dad and Pops will make sure you know how to cook."

"As for Grandma Bell, trust and believe that whenever you visit her, she will have you seated at the kitchen table as soon as you come in the door." Ronnell relaxed on the sofa, joined by Lamar.

"Yeah, it's settled. We're coming here for college," was Allan's conclusion. "We'll just have to suck it up when the winters come, but we can do this."

"Enough said. Tomorrow morning, we call Mom and Dad with the news," Mickey said. "They'll love it."

Chapter 5

Spring 2006

Returning to Nassau after the twins' spring break in Minneapolis only made the Davis family's New Year's Day decision more imperative. With the support of their parents, Allan and Mickey began the process of registration for the fall at the University of Minnesota. Cousin Theo happily continued exercising his influence on their behalf. Although their status as honors students spoke for itself, the twins were concerned that the university's request for transcripts might tip off the wrong people about their plans. Their parents and Okeidi foresaw that possibility, covering their tracks by having them submit applications to numerous colleges and universities. The subsequent barrage of acceptance letters bore evidence of the adults' wisdom.

As the weeks went by, and the time for the senior prom approached, Allan felt a tinge of sadness. He knew he wouldn't be attending. What happened for Uncle Bernie, Uncle Sherman, and Uncle Marty's kids with their prom 19 years ago in Evanston, Illinois was unlikely to take place in Nassau, even though it was the 21st century. The one encouraging note, as Mickey reminded him, was their impending departure. They could turn soon their backs on the place. His brother also added in solidarity, "Besides, if you can't go to the prom, I'm not going either."

On prom night, the Davis twins were conspicuous by their absence. Instead, they booked a flight and spent the weekend in San Juan, Puerto Rico where they partied with relatives of their

Cousin Valentine's husband, Carlos. The hospitality was wonderful and Allan could forget about the issues at home. *It won't be long now. We'll be out of there, and opportunities will really open up for me. But there's one thing I still need to do. It's only right, and I can't put it off much longer. I just need to get through commencement first.*

The commencement ceremony itself placed the school in a quandary. Academically, the twins not only had identical GPAs but the highest GPAs in their graduating class. Faced with that situation, the headmaster, Dr. Collins, made the unprecedented decision of making them co-valedictorians.

"Maybe we should make our speech about the kind of crap you've had to deal with here," Mickey said with bitterness after receiving the news.

"I know. I'm dying to, as Mom and Dad put it, read people the Riot Act—not just for me, but for my fellow classmates who are too scared to do it," Allan agreed. "The thing is, we can do nothing which will call attention to ourselves until Mom and Dad make their announcement. We have to keep this under wraps until then."

"I hate to admit it, but you're right. Mom, Dad, and Okeidi have a plan for all this. If it's going to work, we have to stick to the plan. Still, I really wish we could. You know, we could fall asleep during Collins' speech." Mickey's mouth morphed into a mischievous grin.

Allan, remembering a comment by Dr. Collins that 'Your snoring is enough to wake the dead,' laughed. "Yeah, that would put his drawers in a knot. But Mom and Dad will be there."

"True. Meanwhile, when are you gonna tell him?"

"After commencement."

"You think he'll leak the news?"

Allan ran a hand through his dreadlocks and sighed. "Let's see. Thomas isn't just in the closet; it's a walk-in closet with security locks and climate control, so it's highly unlikely. Still, he's a cop, so just in case..."

Mickey received his twin's unspoken message, giving him a brotha hug. "Gotcha."

Michael and Lissa were seated near the front as other parents arrived for the commencement ceremony on June 16, 2006. Seeing their sons graduate was one of the high points in their lives, and their hearts were full as they watched Allan and Mickey in cap and gown during the processional. The low-key tone of their valedictory speeches came as no surprise, having been apprised of their plans the day before yesterday. When they finally stepped up to receive their diplomas, neither of them was smiling. Although they understood the bigger picture, Michael and Lissa wished their sons could have spoken their truths in those moments. *Oh well, there will be an opportunity for that soon,* Michael thought. *Everyone in the islands will know after we're done. And once we land at O'Hare, the celebration will truly begin.*

The moment the graduating class tossed their caps into the air, Lissa was certain that her twins did so with far more enthusiasm and force than the others, knowing well the reason for it. With the end of the ceremony, she and Michael wasted no time in locating Mickey and Allan, spiriting them off to one of their favorite restaurants for a private celebration. Their plan had now shifted into the final stages.

Allan knew this day would come sooner or later. Part of him was dreading what had to be done while the other part knew this needed to happen in order to move forward. Thomas had been calling him a little more frequently since New Year's Eve, anxious to get together and frustrated by his distance. Allan's response had been noncommittal, subtly giving Thomas a taste of his own medicine.

In retrospect, it had been all right at first, having a hot, sexy police officer interested in him and the steamy encounters they shared. However, the price, in this place, turned out to be too high for his self-respect. With the family departure mere days away, it was imperative to handle this unfinished business.

Uncertain of what Thomas Hamilton was capable of, Allan brought a little added insurance. "Don't worry, bro. I've got your back," Mickey encouraged as they approached the meeting place, finding a spot where he could hear but not be seen as his twin continued on.

Allan watched as Thomas entered the clearing. He had refused to see Thomas unless it was in broad daylight, and his request was reluctantly acknowledged. It must have been his day off, for he was dressed casually in a T-shirt, knee-length walking shorts, and sandals that complemented his rich brown complexion and his well-built, 6'3" body. His semi-erection was evidence he'd gone commando. *Was he honestly thinking we'd hook up?*

Thomas approached Allan with his familiar look of desire, only this time it was mixed with uncertainty as he scanned the area. Allan noticed the way Thomas' eyes dropped to his crotch and the subtle, involuntary licking of his lips as he approached him. Sighing inwardly, he mentally prepared himself.

"Hi, Thomas," Allan said.

"Allan," was Thomas' reply as he went in for an embrace and a deep kiss, puzzled when Allan backed away. "All right. What's going on?"

"There's something I need to tell you."

The wariness in the police officer's eyes became more apparent. "What is it?"

Allan drew a breath. "We're leaving in a few days."

"What do you mean, 'We're leaving'?"

"My family is leaving the Bahamas for good. And I'll be with them."

"Oh. So, it's like that, huh?" Thomas shook his head in denial. "You're just going to up and leave me?"

"Thomas, this wasn't a decision we came to lightly. It was fine for my parents when they first moved here before I was born. But I'm 18, and it's different now. There's no future for me here, and there's no future for us unless I remain your dirty little secret."

"No. You can't leave." Thomas managed to drum up some authority in his voice despite the shock. "I want you here."

Allan had expected Thomas' response, yet he retained all the self-control he could muster while delivering his message. "We've gone through this all before, Thomas. I have never hidden who I am. Being with you under all your rigid conditions is no longer acceptable. It hurts. You're hot, I'll give you that, but your fear is stronger than your wanting to be with me openly. I already know you won't leave these islands to be with me, either. I'm not here to force you to come out, but I refuse to argue with you anymore. What you choose to do with your life is on you, but I'm moving on. Let's just put a good face on it and say goodbye."

"No! I won't let you! You're mine!" Thomas commanded. "If you go, I'll…"

"You'll what?" Allan asked calmly. He could hear Mickey walking up behind him. Thomas' body went from tense anger to nervous tics.

Suspicious and paranoid, Thomas looked from one twin to the other. "What's he doing here?"

"I know everything about you and my brother. I'm here to make sure you don't give him any trouble." Mickey's face was all business. "What I heard just now sounded like a threat."

"Since you've been throwing my pedigree in my face lately, let me tell you a few things." Allan stepped back and to Mickey's side. "My family has my back, and I love them for it. I'm named after my grandfather. He was rather homophobic when he was younger, but he came around, and he's a better person for it. I can talk to him about anything. And he—in fact, all the elders in this big family—taught us a lot about family unity. They love me for the person I am."

"So, Thomas, if you plan on doing anything to hurt Allan, know this," Mickey continued, voice firm but not raised. "You won't have just me and our parents after you. You'll have the entire Christopher family after you and everything that goes with it."

"By the way, our parents are expecting us back in an hour. If we're not, they know what to do." Allan looked at the handsome man standing before him whose face was now a mixture of fear and impotent anger. He almost felt pity for Thomas. Maybe one day more people would live and speak their truths here, but Allan knew he would only witness that from a distance.

Thomas' shoulders finally slumped. He was beaten, and he knew it. Granted, he had grown accustomed to the authority a police officer carried. Now, his façade had cracked, and he was face to face with his own cowardliness and shame. The medicine was bitter; it had cost him someone he had grown to care about. When he found his voice, it was pleading. "Allan, isn't there—"

"No, Thomas. It's over. You and I are done."

Thomas could only watch in despair as Allan and Mickey left the clearing. Though Allan's parting words resounded in his mind, his body had not received the memo. The police officer's dick was stiff in his shorts, his hole aching with the need to be filled, need for someone who was now lost to him forever. A young man with charming "Beckley eyes" he could have only in his memory.

"I know that was tough for you," Mickey said as they drove back to Nassau. "Hey, if a woman was draining me the way he did you, I probably would have done the same thing."

"You know, I thought that because he was older, things would be different. Guess I was wrong."

"If Thomas chose fear over you, he didn't deserve you in the first place with his cowardly ass. He really needs to grow a pair." Mickey squeezed Allan's shoulder. "Just by being who you are, you're way braver and stronger than he'll ever be."

"Thanks, Mickey."

On the return trip, the conversation between the twins turned to college, pleased over their admittance to the U of M with honors. The thought of making new friends was appealing, as well as blending into a much larger population—well, as much as they could. When they arrived and entered the villa, Allan felt taller and a bit stronger.

"It's done," Allan said in response to the unspoken question on the faces of his parents.

"How do you feel?" Lissa asked.

"Well, sad on one hand that it didn't work out, but relieved on the other. Does that make sense?"

Michael put a comforting arm around his son. "Yes, it does. Breakups are never easy. You'll feel what you feel, and you just have to take it one day at a time. Like we've said before, there is someone out there who's right for you. A man who is worthy of you and your heart."

"Exactly. And we're always here for you, Allan," Lissa added as the family came together for a group hug.

Okeidi issued the press release the next day, which was followed up by an exclusive radio interview with Lissa and Michael. They could have opted to simply say that it was time for them to return to the U.S. Instead, Michael told the interviewer, "When we first came here, we felt welcomed and appreciated as artists and performers. That, however, has changed. We have always stood for equality, love, and acceptance, especially for our sons, no matter who they love. We don't see that happening here. As you know, they're identical twins. Yet, one of them is welcomed and embraced, while the other is barely tolerated. As parents, we find that unacceptable."

"But the U.S. seems to be having those problems as well," the host countered.

"That may very well be, but we have a strong, supportive family there, and though things seem to be moving slowly, they are changing," Lissa replied, keeping to herself the vision Cousin Eli had when they visited Minneapolis a couple of months ago. They had been discussing Sunrise's latest concert when Cousin Eli got a certain look in his eye. Lissa stopped talking and waited for him to come back from his vision. When he did, he said, "It will take time, possibly years, but a movement called marriage equality will become the law of the land, not only in other countries, but in the U.S., where it's just beginning." Lissa, like the rest of the Christopher family, knew that no matter how long it took, Cousin Eli's visions always came to pass. The knowledge spurred her on as she and Michael continued to speak from confidence and conviction for the remainder of the interview.

It was no surprise that their interview made the local news stations, which in turn became fodder for gossip and dialogue throughout the islands. Lissa and Michael also received their share of phone calls about their decision, most of which they referred to Okeidi. Business owners whose livelihood had been boosted from having the international celebrities in residence now grew nervous. No doubt, the ones who were the most worried were those who had snubbed Allan. Media sources picked up the story and plastered it across the Internet. Loyal Sunrise fans were outraged over the treatment of someone they considered one of their own. Elected officials were caught in the crossfire. All in all, it was a public relations nightmare for the islands. The Davis family had struck where it hurt the most—in the wallet.

In the meantime, with days to go before their departure, closing up shop and packing their personal belongings was well under way, and their cars had already been shipped. Regardless of the reason, it was still a little difficult for Allan to move from a place he'd lived in all his life—deciding what to take, what to give away, what to donate. Memories he had of growing up on the islands were now tinged with a bittersweet quality.

Mickey had had his share of problems as well, the most recent of which was a young woman there who vehemently claimed she was pregnant with his baby. Oddly enough, this news surfaced just after the press release. Allan knew in his heart the claim was false, and subsequent tests done by their family doctor plus an independent doctor confirmed it.

"I knew it," Mickey declared emphatically while they were finishing their packing. "You know how I roll. There was no way it could have been mine. And the kicker? She wasn't even pregnant!"

"It sucks, I know," Allan concurred. "The good thing about all this is that the truth came out, and there were no surprises."

"Yeah. The sooner we get out of here the better. By the way, is everything on board for Ms. Bond?"

"All set. She has her visa."

Mickey looked down the hall in the direction of Ms. Bond's suite, reflecting on the petite, sepia brown, middle-aged woman who had been a significant part of his life, almost as much as his parents. "Good. It wouldn't be the same without her."

"Tell me about it. She smacked you upside your head while she told you, 'That's what can happen to you when you don't keep it in your pants!' But you know as well as I do it's all because she cares about you."

Mickey laughed, for the first time since the scam broke. "That she does. Just like when she told you, 'You don't need some grown man hiding under the bed. You can do much better than that.'"

"Touche'. Not everyone here suffers from narrow-mindedness."

The twins were silent for a few moments, sharing that inner communication of their memories of Nassau before they returned to the sorting and packing tasks before them.

Three days later, Allan and his family were gathered at the airport, awaiting their morning flight. "We'll be there to meet you with lots of hugs and plenty of love, Little Allan," his grandfather told him when he called the night before. He found himself thinking about life back in the U.S. again, which strangely led him to thoughts of Thomas. It had been difficult to say the words, but he knew in his heart it was necessary in order to move on. *Who knows? Maybe one day this place will enter the 21st century when it comes to LGBT folks. Stranger things have happened.*

When their flight was called for boarding, the Davis family regarded one another in quiet understanding and took their places in line, accompanied by Ms. Bond. They stretched out in their first-class seats as the flight attendant gave the usual spiel. Lissa gave her husband a friendly look, one which also admonished him to stay awake for the flight by any means necessary. Michael merely nodded and shrugged his shoulders, pulling out a biography of Bob Marley and putting on headphones. Lissa, Mickey, and Allan all had their favorite reading material in hand. Before the plane taxied down the runway, they held hands in prayer and a goodbye. When the plane took off, a new chapter in their lives had already begun…

Chapter 6

Summer 2006

As the plane made its final approach to O'Hare International Airport on June 24, the Davis family was filled with anticipation and familiarity. They were back in the Windy City. There was no doubt in their minds there would be quite a reception once they went through customs, from the family, the band members, and of course, Okeidi.

Thanks to the efforts of Mother and her sisters, their new home was furnished and decorated to their satisfaction; Lissa could hardly wait to see the results. Ronnell Hayes, of course, had overseen the renovations for the recording studio, keeping Michael up to speed and gratified with Michael's approval of the finished product. Since Mr. Garvey wished to remain in Nassau, Lissa and Michael rewarded him for his years of support, loyalty, and faithful service to the family by selling him the villa, furnishings and all, for an extremely reasonable price.

"We're home," Michael said while the plane taxied to the gate.

"Yes." Lissa squeezed her husband's hand and gave him a warm smile. "Yes, we are."

"You know, honey, living on the islands was beautiful, and it worked for us for a long time, but there was always something about Chi-town."

"I know. Sooner or later, we had to come back." She looked behind her at her sons and Ms. Bond, the excitement evident in their eyes.

An abundance of smiles and love from Davises, Christophers, and the Sunrise ensemble greeted the family once they left the customs area. They had always received a warm welcome whenever they visited, but for Lissa, there was something extra now; this marked a welcome back into the fold. Returning to Chicago had been the right decision at the right time, and she gratefully savored the moment.

A certain number of flashing cameras and media presence awaited their arrival as well, all looking for a sound bite. In response, the Davis family merely smiled, said a few words, and moved on to the waiting limo while Allan Beckley Christopher had members of his staff secure their luggage. "I know you want to see your new place and relax a bit, but we'll see you all at the estate tonight." Grinning from ear to ear, he gave his daughter an affectionate hug. "It's great to have you back, Allison."

"Thanks, Father. It's great to be back."

During the chauffeur's navigation of the Tri-State Tollway and the Ronald Reagan Tollway to their destination, Ms. Bond could only gawk at the sheer volume of traffic. "I have never seen anything like this," she gasped.

"If you think this is something, wait until you see the Loop," Allan told her.

"What is the Loop?"

"That's what we call downtown Chicago. Stores, skyscrapers, and all. Actually, from what I've read, Chicago is three times the size of New Providence Island in land area."

Mickey gave her a mischievous smile. "We won't see the Loop today, but face it, Ms. Bond, you're not in Nassau anymore."

"Sons," Michael gently chided them. "Let's not overwhelm Ms. Bond. We're almost home, so let's chill."

When they walked through the door of their new three-story home on Sunset Avenue in Glen Ellyn, one of the affluent western suburbs in DuPage County, Lissa glowed with satisfaction. It was by no means near the level of their villa in Nassau, but it held a certain charm of its own thanks to the special touches Mother made sure were added to it, like the family photos and the artwork of the islands.

Five bedrooms and a four-car garage were quite sufficient for their needs, not to mention the state-of-the-art kitchen, spacious walk-in closets for each bedroom, and a lower level that been remodeled into a family area and a soundproofed studio. Ms. Bond had her own suite, and though the twins had their bedrooms for now, Lissa could easily visualize converting them into a sewing room for herself and a "man cave" for Michael once their sons moved out.

That evening, at the Christopher estate in Evanston, they were treated to a lavish welcome-home party attended by their extended family and a select number of invited guests. In a way, it reminded Lissa of Father's 60th birthday party, only with a much happier ending. Closer to the truth was the promise she made years ago, before Sunrise locked onto the trajectory of success it now enjoyed: to stay rooted and grounded with those who were there from the very beginning. Surrounded by the familiar faces at the party, she was exceedingly thankful she'd kept that promise.

She beamed at Okeidi, who had taken her aside for a private moment. "We are so grateful to you for all you did to help us, so we could get out of there. And we're thrilled to be back."

"You know I've got you, Lissa," Okeidi replied. "Nobody, I mean *nobody,* hurts those boys. Not on my watch. How have they been?"

"All things considered, they're holding up well. Mickey is free of that island tart who tried to trap him. Allan is taking a break from dating, but here he has a better chance at finding a man who deserves him. You already know how it is in this business. It's going to take time. Besides, they'll be going up to the Twin Cities for college in the fall, and that will keep them busy. By the way, how's Malkia handling her new role in the business?"

Okeidi preened with pride over the daughter she was grooming to take over her agency. "She is running with it. By the way, Sunrise's engagement at McCormick Place is already sold out. Your fans are primed and ready for your return. But we can discuss business later. Your homecoming celebration comes first."

In another part of the estate, Allan was engaged in conversation with his Uncle Sammy. True to their word, Sammy and Darnell had flown in from California for the big homecoming, and Allan couldn't have been happier.

"Tell me what's going on at the ranch."

Sammy played coy. "Like what, Little Allan?"

"You know what I'm talking about. Is Uncle Bernie going to go out there and work with you or not?"

"Well, I hope he does," Sammy admitted. "We could certainly use him out there. His skills as a DVM would be an asset to the ranch and my practice."

"Yeah. Not only that, you'd have some more family out there with you, as well as your ranch family."

"True. He said he'd discuss it with your Uncle Sherman, so I expect to hear something from them soon one way or the other." Sammy gave his grandnephew a fond smile. "And now that you're free from a gay 'jail sentence,' what's in store for you?"

"To have fun over the summer, go off to the U of M, get my degree, and take my time about finding the right guy."

"That's the spirit, Little Allan. And I wish you every success."

"Thanks, Uncle Sammy," Allan replied, giving him a hug.

The next few weeks were a whirlwind of reconnecting with their huge family, summer fun, and rehearsals for the upcoming concert. Michael wasted no time breaking in the new studio with Sunrise. Mickey would rehearse with them from time to time, and Lissa's voice was clear and finely tuned with the wealth of experience. For all his ability with lyrics, Allan knew he could carry a tune about as well as Lucy Ricardo, for which he was occasionally teased. It served as one of the ways people who knew them could tell him apart from Mickey. Still, he loved to watch, silently cheering them on.

July's performance at the Arie Crown Theatre section of McCormick Place was Old Home Week to the ensemble, and it was a rush having a mix of loyal fans and new fans in the audience. When the curtain went up, the audience response was deafening.

Lissa sang with the joy in her heart of being home again. With the intimate musical knowledge of each other that only comes from years of performing, Sunrise's opening night was a *bona fide* success. Of course, her parents, her children, and her extended family were seated in the VIP section. Michael and Ronnell had introduced a lot of new material into the concert, which was well received. Their hits, like "Afro Mystic" and "Indies Blues," were included in their musical selection. Due to the publicity generated by their radio interview prior to their return to Chicago, their Grammy-winning song "The Right to Be" became a huge fan request once again.

Afterwards, the Sunrise entourage—which now included Sol and Medford's families—went straight to the Funky Frogway for their after-concert meal, high on an electrifying performance. Chico, the owner, moved by their loyalty, always greeted them like visiting royalty but seasoned with down-home common sense. The coffeehouse had become an institution in the New Town neighborhood, and the warmth Chico and his children provided when customers walked through the doors ensured regular business. After biting into juicy, spicy, sinfully delicious steakburgers, Allan and Mickey conceded the wisdom of their parents' support of the establishment over the past 30-plus years.

The end of August arrived in a mere blink. Lissa and Michael knew the time had come for their sons to test their wings with college. Emotionally, they were reminded of the twins' first day in kindergarten. Lissa simply couldn't get through rehearsal that day. Michael went through the motions, but he was far from his usual Mr. Precision. Opting to cut rehearsal short, Michael took two packages of popcorn from a kitchen cupboard and popped one into the microwave oven while Lissa poured two glasses of mango juice on the rocks.

No words were needed once they settled into their master bedroom and a DVD was dropped into the player. The images which appeared on the flat screen television brought a pull to their hearts from long ago. "Look at them," Lissa gushed. "They're having so much fun building that sandcastle. How old were they?"

"Seven, I think." Michael broke out into a laugh at the next scene.

"And there you are, planting the flag like a conquering hero."

"Well, what can I say?" Michael finished munching some kernels of popcorn and assumed a mock-bragging pose. "You know, through it all, we raised some amazing kids."

"Don't let them hear you say kids," Lissa teased as further family videos played across the screen. "But you're right, honey. We've given them the tools; now it's time for them to go out on their own. I just wish they could have been kids for a little while longer."

"I know, Lissa." Michael held his wife tenderly as her tears mingled with his own. "I know."

With both their Range Rovers loaded, Allan and Mickey headed up Interstate 90, stopping for lunch in Madison, Wisconsin before they resumed their journey via Interstate 94 to the Twin Cities. Their father had taught them well the importance of knowing how to read a map and learning a city. In his words, "GPS may be a good tool, but it doesn't know everything." Wisconsin's dairy country had a charm of its own; while they passed through the Wisconsin Dells area in Sauk County, Allan made a note to visit the waterparks in the future.

The music playing on the CD was his speed. The countryside was conducive to a relaxing drive, yet Allan found his mind going back to a certain police officer on the islands—again. For all his outer façade of toughness, command, and control, he remembered the fear on Thomas' face when he left the clearing that day in mid-June. Sure, he couldn't force Thomas to come out before he was ready. However, he'd been witness to the loving relationships of his LGBT relatives, and what he thought he had with Thomas fell short. It didn't mean moving on would be easy but, as his parents and Uncle Sammy had told him, he could only take things one day at a time.

"Honey hush, they're back," Cousin Wayne exclaimed as he and Cousin Theo greeted the twins upon their arrival in the late afternoon. "Now get on in here. Everything's already set up, so you can just lay back and relax. How are your folks?"

"They're good, but I think this has been harder on them than it is on us," Mickey mused, remembering how his parents did their level best to refrain from crying during their goodbyes; he and Allan had mist in their eyes as well. "The same with Ms. Bond."

"I hope you remember that when you become a parent," Cousin Theo admonished.

"Hey, we're only 18. Give us some slack," Allan protested.

"Anyway, let's get these cars unloaded so we can sit down, eat, and dish." Cousin Wayne proceeded to grab a suitcase, followed suit by Cousin Theo and the twins.

"Where's Ronnell and Jermaine?" Mickey picked up one of his backpacks.

"They'll be here shortly. They're bringing dinner guests."

As one who faithfully viewed cycle upon cycle of *America's Next Top Model,* meeting Ronnell and Jermaine's guests that evening was unexpected *déjà vu* for Allan. Hari Langley and Dylan Spencer were younger, gay versions of Tyson Beckford and Nigel Barker. Hari stood at 5'9", sporting the well-defined build of a track star, grey eyes, a modified Afro, and a skin tone two shades lighter than the famous supermodel. Dylan was 5'11", with an athletic build suitable for rugby. There was a twinkle in his hazel eyes, and unlike the real Nigel Barker, he had chosen to keep his long, luxurious mane. Then there was the way they looked at one another, the way only couples do. *Well, well, well.*

"It's a pleasure to meet you, Allan." Dylan shook his hand. Allan swore he was in the Twilight Zone at the sound of that flawless British accent. "Your cousins talk about you a lot."

Allan glanced over at said cousins before he shook Hari's hand. "I can imagine."

"Did you ever go on tour with Sunrise?"

"Only until we were five. After that, they made sure we were in school and kept us on a normal routine. It wasn't easy when they were off on tour, but they always made sure to call us every day while they were gone. You know, I feel like you two just walked off the set of my favorite TV show, but I'm sure you get that a lot."

"We do," Hari agreed. "People keep insisting we should be models. The thing is, we're not into that."

"Do you ever watch the show?"

"My sister wouldn't let us alone, so we gave in and started watching it a couple of cycles ago," Dylan replied. "We know the mean girls never win, so we like to see what challenge or photo shoot they'll come up with next."

Hari laughed. "As for my sisters, Latryce enjoys the journey to the top two and the different countries they travel to. They both do. But Sharian lives for, as she puts it, the screaming, the drama, and the cat claws."

Dylan took Hari's hand, giving it an affectionate squeeze. "When we first started dating, and Philippa found out that Hari's sisters are huge fans of the show, that sealed it for her. They are practically inseparable." Dylan indicated Mickey. "Do you watch *America's Next Top Model?*"

"I watch it but only when the competition is down to the final two. I like *Forensic Files, Cold Cases, Midsomer Murders,* and the *Law and Order* franchise," Mickey replied. "So, do you go to the U of M?"

"Macalester College," Hari said, his eyes adoring Dylan. "Actually, that's where we met. It was sophomore year last spring. I was running sprints around the track, and Dylan was sitting in the bleachers. He couldn't take his eyes off me."

"Well, before I tell you two to get a room, it's time to see Tyra," Jermaine broke in.

After the episode ended, the young men engaged in a recap discussion of the boot camp torture the models endured for the photo shoot, fueled by the verbal catfights in the house. At least, that was what the models thought it was, those who had the woefully naïve notion that all one needed to do was stand and look pretty for photos. Though he had only known their guests a few hours, Allan felt like he was among old friends.

"You know, I can imagine the kind of stuff you've been through as a couple—from the outside, I mean," Allan told Hari and Dylan.

Hari raised an eyebrow. "You're very perceptive."

"When my Uncle Josh and my Aunt Penny were dating, they had their challenges. Aunt Penny looks like Elizabeth Taylor. People tried to break them up, not because they wanted them but because they wanted them away from each other. The LGBT community is no different, even here."

"I've dated African American guys, Latino guys, white guys," Hari mused. "When it came to white guys, before Dylan, there was a certain pattern there. They were down for a hook-up or a fling, but I wasn't considered good enough to meet their friends. And for those who were 'into Black men,' I had to question their motives. Like, are you with me in spite of my color or because of my color? Was I some fulfillment of a fantasy?"

"I get it. How about you, Dylan?"

Dylan thought for a second. "Well, Mum is like Her Majesty. She looks at character first. She taught us never to judge, find out if the man is interesting enough to date, and get to know him first. That's what happened with me and Hari, and over the course of time, we fell in love. Where Dad's concerned, if a man treats me right, that's what counts. As for some of my white so-called friends, when they found out I was seeing Hari, they'd ask me questions like, 'Why are you with him?' when he wasn't around. I knew what they were implying. Needless to say, I told them what's what and dropped them like yesterday's fish and chips. Those who are truly our friends have remained so, like Ronnell and his mate and Jermaine. And Philippa has always been in my corner; she lays down the law with any man she dates."

"Yeah, I can tell it." Ronnell took a sip of vitamin water. "Vicious queens tried to stir up mess to break them up, but they weren't having it."

Hari's eyes locked on Allan. "Now, spill. What's going on in your love life?"

"I'm taking a break from boyfriends for now. I just want to concentrate on school, friends, family. Besides, dating is a little more complicated for Mickey and me."

"Because of who your parents are?"

"Exactly."

When it came to the dating pool and college life, Allan and Mickey were considered fair game, as they soon discovered after freshman orientation. Coeds were everywhere, throwing themselves at the twins. After the pregnancy scam, Mickey was friendly and polite but selective when playing the field. He did hang out with women but more in a friendly, group-activities way. Allan also received this unwanted attention from said women, from flirting to sometimes brazen propositions. Before things could progress any further, he responded with a polite "Sorry, but I play for the other team." That was enough to get the message across. As added insurance, he purchased a rainbow necklace and bracelet to wear wherever he went.

The men were another story. It was encouraging to have guys around who owned who they were and made no apologies for it; that, he could appreciate. His "Beckley eyes" and his looks, on the other hand, did attract a certain number of guys who saw him merely as a hook-up fantasy. Drawing on the experiences of his parents, he was able to weed out those predators for the most part, preferring to hang out with his Edwards cousins on the occasions when they went out dancing and gradually making a few select friends on campus.

Given the fact Sunrise's fan base consisted of older aficionados, the twins' life as freshman college students operated under the radar, made easier by the university's huge student population. That is, until Sunrise was booked to play Minneapolis in February. The tickets didn't sell out in minutes like a Barbra Streisand concert, but they did sell out quickly.

"I have to give it to Ms. Frazier. Orchestra Hall is packed for the duration of their engagement," Allan said after ending the call with his parents. "But it'll be good to see them." He turned to Cousin Wayne. "You can tell Cousin Brian and Cousin Theo that Malkia took care of everything. VIP tickets, backstage passes, the works."

"Honey hush," Cousin Wayne beamed. "They won't be able to sit still until opening night. Are you two bringing dates?"

"Probably not. Actually, it's better not to bring a date to a concert my parents are headlining. At least, not yet. Know what I mean?"

Cousin Wayne nodded in understanding. "That can't be easy for you, Allan. But you still have your family here to enjoy the concert with."

"Heeyyyy." Ronnell sashayed into the family room, giving imaginary wind to his lion's mane of hair, inspired by Diana Ross. Not only did he love the fact that he and Miss J shared the same skin tone, but he had been taking tips from the diva on how to work every walkway like a runway.

"Hey Cuz. How did you do on the exam?"

Ronnell stopped, blew on his glitter-painted nails, and gave them his best Pepsodent smile. "Fierce."

"That's my princess," Cousin Wayne teased proudly. "Do I see another Dean's List report on the way?"

"Daddy, I will take up permanent residence on the Dean's List. RuPaul says 'You Better Work,' 'cause that's what it took to get those grades."

"Does that mean you and Lamar will be free on Sunrise's opening night here?" Allan asked.

Ronnell gave them his best hair toss. "Now you know I must have a new outfit for that."

On opening night, Allan, Mickey, and the Edwards family were seated in the VIP section of Orchestra Hall, surrounded by cheering Sunrise fans. Still not acclimated to winter in Minnesota, the twins were bundled up in layers of thermal underwear, turtlenecks, sweaters, and wool socks. They could elude cameras only so long, but Okeidi, as always, found a way to spin things. "Now, when anyone asks, you can just say you wanted to come up and see your parents' concert here. You've done this before when you've had time off from school, so no one should suspect that you're living here."

"And because most Sunrise fans are Mom and Dad's age," Mickey concluded.

"You catch on quick. And Eli and Madear have briefed everyone here to corroborate it."

Allan had attended many a Sunrise opening night, but he always loved the magical quality about them. Surrounded by his Edwards and Bell relatives, the rush was there, the energy and synergy that made Sunrise legendary. Cousin Brian and Cousin Theo were starstruck; if they had been his age, he was sure Cousin Brian would have gone total fanboy on Sunrise after the concert. Mickey, of course, was immersed in the zone of the music, thinking of how he would blend his riffs into the instrumentals, given the opportunity.

At the end of the concert, the twins and the rest of the family happily joined Sunrise backstage, followed by a trip to the Edwards mansion to celebrate a successful night. Although there were some reporters on hand before they left, Allan and Mickey worked Okeidi's advice to the letter. There was a tense moment with Cousin Brian, when a reporter approached him; fortunately, he pulled it together when Cousin Clarissa gave him a look. Breathing in relief once they were out of range of cameras and microphones, Allan was comforted that for now, their secret was safe.

Chapter 7

Spring 2007

At last—*at last*—winter gave way to spring. Aside from the Sunrise concert, Allan thought he'd literally been in study hibernation, rarely taking his head out from a book or a laptop. All his college-age cousins, in fact, suffered from this peculiar strain of cabin fever, each beyond ready for socializing during spring break. *Hmmm. This could be the time to test the dating waters again. Nothing hot and heavy, but fun.*

When he came home after his latest date on a Friday night in April, all Allan wanted to do was soak in the tub and call it a night. On campus, Shakir Delray appeared to have it going on since he was a senior and on track for his business degree. The brotha was handsome and smart, with just enough of a bad-boy vibe to tweak his sex appeal. Allan, bowing to Shakir's confident persistence, had agreed to go out with him in the hopes of getting to know him better.

The 90s, however, was hardly a place he would have chosen for a first date. The music was loud enough to prevent any serious conversation. Shakir's "thug clothes" set him back for a second, but who was he to judge? What was harder to ignore was the amount of alcohol he consumed and the way Shakir was constantly pushing up on him and grabbing his package while they danced.

Reluctantly, Allan had to admit he'd missed the mark. This guy was only interested in getting in his drawers, probably before they even left the club. Finally, at a point when he became the recipient of yet another spilled drink, Allan managed to load the intoxicated

Shakir into a cab and sent him on his way. As the cab pulled away, he could hear Shakir's drunken rants of, "You want me! I know you want me!"

"Hey," he heard Mickey say. "How was your date?"

Allan collapsed onto his bed. "Don't ask. Wait. Strike that. This will be another one in my portfolio of bad dates."

Mickey sat up. "All right. Spill."

Allan toed off his shoes, kicked them to the side, and sighed. "It was like this guy was one person on campus and a whole different person when we went out. He took me to the 90s for our date. It went downhill from there, to the point where he was literally all over me."

"I've dated women like that," Mickey commiserated. "So, where is he? And what's with the booze I smell? You don't drink."

"The last I saw of him, I put his drunk ass in a cab after he spilled his share of drinks on me. It was one thing to have not enough in Nassau, but this is a bit too much."

"Maybe, but you still have a better chance of finding a guy here than you ever could there. How does the story go? You kissed a frog this time."

"The folks keep saying there's no rush. I just have to find someone who balances things out." Allan managed a smile, the first he'd had that evening. "Or maybe he'll find me."

"There you go." Mickey gave his twin a high-five.

"Speaking of dating, what's going on with you?"

"I'm going out with Marchelle tomorrow, but I'm keeping things cool. Date, have fun, flirt, but after that shit show with Tara back on the island, no hookups. At least, for now."

"Smart. Anyway, I need a shower. This experience with Shakir reminded me of one thing."

"What's that?"

"I may want it, but I'm not desperate."

Mickey gave him another high-five. "There you go! We're the Davis twins."

A couple of weeks later, Allan finished his last class of the day, long strides taking him across campus past Northrop Auditorium to one of the parking lots. "Hey! Allan!" he heard a voice call out behind him. "Wait up!"

Allan stopped and turned, his face falling when he realized who it was. "Oh. Hey, Shakir."

"Man, can we talk for a sec? I've been trying to get up the nerve to tell you something."

"I don't know what we would have to talk about after –"

"That's just it. I fucked up. I know I fucked up, getting all wasted and grabbing on you. I'm sorry I did that. Allan, I want a do-over. Just give me a chance to show you I'm better than that."

Allan was skeptical. "I don't know…"

"Please?" Shakir begged. "I promise, no bars this time."

Allan looked down at Shakir thoughtfully. *He seems so sincere about it. Maybe I can give him the benefit of the doubt this once.* "OK, how about a movie?"

Shakir gave him a humble smile, although it was just below the megawatt level. "Cool. Let's make it Saturday night."

Saturday evening was a comfortable one for spring, and Allan was more relaxed after finishing his homework assignments while he drove to the apartment complex in southeast Minneapolis, where Shakir was waiting for him outside. *He cleaned up well,* Allan admitted to himself; his look was on the collegiate side this time.

Mickey, Bradley, and Rico, who planned for an evening at the roller rink, were skeptical about this second date. "From what you told me about this dude, he may have apologized, but I'm still not sure about him," Mickey stated. Allan, however, believed that a man's word was his bond, though he acknowledged their words of caution.

With the moderate traffic on I-94, they soon pulled up to the metroplex theatre in Brooklyn Center, a working-class suburb north of Minneapolis. By this time, Allan felt more comfortable around Shakir, who was most charming. Sure, Shakir seemed a bit guarded when asked about his family and friends, but he made up for it by holding Allan's hand in public while they walked to the theatre. Besides, Allan knew he was keeping his own family background under wraps as well. After a stop at the concession stand, they found their seats with a huge bucket of popcorn to share and large sodas for the duration of the movie—plus Twizzlers on the side.

The movie was a highly engaging whodunit, with the murder victim a high-profile newscaster. Aside from side comments here and there with Shakir and squeezing his hand from time to time, Allan's attention was locked onto the screen. He even snacked and drank his Dr. Pepper without taking his eyes away. *The way Mickey watches* Midsomer Murders, *he'd love this.* The list of suspects grew, the motives mounted, while Allan remained thoroughly engrossed.

Halfway through the movie, just as a vital clue was revealed through a second inspection of the crime scene, strangeness settled into Allan's body. Concentration was difficult. He nodded off when he knew he'd had plenty of rest. His brain seemed to be in a London fog. What was going on?

At the Roller Garden that evening, Mickey was enjoying the music, and the mood on his custom-made skates, flirting with the young women who came out for the evening and embracing the camaraderie of another one of his third cousins, Lucius Bradley Edwards, and Lucius' new boyfriend, Rico McDonald. Jennifer Hudson's "Love You I Do" was the current selection, and he couldn't resist showing off his skating skills. He weaved. He spun with dreadlocks flying. He danced. He even clowned to smiles and cheers. However, in the midst of all the fun, an unsettling feeling took root.

Something was wrong. More to the point, something was wrong with his twin.

Allan had no memory of time passing, yet he still found it difficult to focus. It was as though he was outside his body, watching himself say no, but his body having other ideas as he felt his dick being stroked. The space surrounding him smelled older, more confined. Why was he laying on his back? Movie seats weren't like that. Sure, he was responding to the stimulation, yet his voice kept saying no. And his resistance was nil.

Why is that? Why is it so quiet? And why am I naked?

Bradley glided effortlessly on the skating floor with Rico, enjoying the song and his company. Jennifer Hudson's music had everyone up and partying. Being one of her fans, he considered it his sworn duty to send positive energy her way. Rico, the only person allowed to call him Lucius, was more than happy to support him, knowing how well he would be rewarded once they were home. One moment they were doing a well-choreographed couple's skate. The next…

"Lucius. What's going on?" Rico asked, concerned over the zoned-out look in his eyes. Not getting a response, Rico carefully guided him off the floor to a spot where they could sit.

"Allan," Bradley finally uttered when he came back from where he'd been. "Rico, we have to get out of here. Where's Mickey?"

"Out on the floor. Why?"

"Just go get him," Bradley urged.

"All right."

Bradley was still processing the vision he experienced when Rico returned with a sweaty, concerned Mickey behind him.

"What's going on, Cuz? What's this about Allan?"

Bradley shook at the thought. "Allan's in trouble. He's been drugged. Someone is planning to…"

Mickey's pupils dilated, and his fists clenched in protective anger. "Oh, shit. Could you see where he is?"

Bradley closed his eyes for a moment. "Yes. We need to go. Now."

Shakir feasted his eyes possessively upon the nude young man lying semiconscious on his bed in his studio apartment, as hot as Dwayne "The Rock" Johnson in every department. Allan's sexy dreads only made him hotter. Lust filled his body, a heat that refused to be ignored while he stroked Allan's huge, thick, lubricated penis. It was two shades darker than the rest of his body, as was his hole, and the contrast made Shakir hotter. He had always believed that big feet meant a big dick, and judging from Allan's size 14s, he didn't disappoint.

He laughed, a soft yet predatory laugh. How easy it was to slip the GHB into Allan's soda under the guise of the dark theater while his attention was superglued to the screen. And Allan put up no resistance when Shakir took him out of the theater, driving his Range Rover back here.

Yes, he had wanted Allan since he first saw him on campus, and he had been determined to get him by any means necessary, once he was away from his entourage of friends and relatives. Getting drunk had been a huge mistake, but not this time. This time, Allan was his to do whatever he wanted, and Shakir wanted to feel all that dick deep inside him, filling him up to sublime satisfaction as he rode it to an orgasm. After that, Allan's big, well rounded, plump ass would be his for the taking. Sure, Shakir was a big man in his own right, but he was average compared to Allan. He knew he would wind up with more than he could handle should Allan fight him off. Hence, the GHB.

Of course, he had to make sure to keep up his borderline hypermasculine front. No one around here could ever know that Shakir Delray liked to take the dick as well as give it. His macho swagger was such that brothas were more than willing to bottom for him in a heartbeat, and he always got his way. Whenever he did bottom, Shakir made sure the hookup was well out of town. But Allan Davis—tall, dreadlocked, gorgeous, built-like-a-brick-house Allan Davis—had been a temptation that was plain impossible to resist. Now, he was finally going to get the dick he'd been craving, and his own deep bronze dick throbbed at the thought while his hole twitched with anticipation.

Reluctantly, he released Allan's manhood to search for the XXL condoms he bought earlier that day. Despite Allan's moans and the slurred "No" that left his lips, his dick was on hard and pulsing. Shakir loved it, seeing this man helpless against anything that was going to happen to him. He found his box of condoms and set it near the bed. *I'll take care of this in a moment.* Grabbing the bottle of lube by his nightstand, he coated his fingers with it before bringing them into the valley between his own bubble butt. *I'm gonna need a lot of lube to take all that,* he observed lustfully as his fingers stretched and prepped his tight hole.

His heated dick was already leaking as he tore open a packet and carefully rolled the condom down Allan's majestic monument to manhood. Now fully relaxed and well past mere horniness, Shakir grabbed Allan's dick at the base and lowered himself until he felt the head at the entrance to his needy hole, ready to fill him. *Now you're mine...*

"You get the fuck off my brother!" Mickey roared as he and his cousins stormed the apartment. Completely taken by surprise, Shakir found himself snatched up and hurled across the room, where he was promptly held at bay by Bradley and Rico.

"So, thought you were going to get a piece of my cousin, huh?" Bradley growled at the sight of Shakir sprawled out awkwardly on the floor, his throbbing erection and well-lubed hole on full display. "Not happening."

Shakir, in an attempt to bluster his way through his aborted plans and cursing himself for failing to lock the front door, quickly got up to launch an attack on Bradley. "Get the fuck out of my place, you motherfu..." he cursed, only to be knocked out by a right cross to his chin by Rico.

"Allan, you're safe," Mickey said. "You're safe. This dude will never mess with you again."

"Mickey," Allan slurred.

"Yeah, it's me. Bradley and Rico are here. Let's get you dressed and out of this place."

"What do we do about him?" Rico indicated the unconscious Shakir. "Should we call the cops?"

"Right now, we need to get Allan out of here." Mickey helped Allan into his clothes. "He can't make any decisions until that drug wears off. We can tell him what happened then. I don't want this dude to get away with what he did any more than you do, but it's still my brother's call. Hopefully, he'll want to include Mom and Dad in this."

A vengeful frown spread across Rico's face. "You know, we could put a dildo up his ass, tie him to the bed, and take pictures. He's already prepped for it."

Bradley, who had been gathering information from the apartment, paused. "Baby, I get how you feel about this rat bastard right now, but then we'd be no better than his sorry ass. Let's just get Allan home and wait for that drug to wear off. That way he can decide what he wants to do."

Mickey, having managed to get his twin fully dressed, was all for that. "Come on. We're out of here."

Although the rape had been prevented, the fact that Shakir had gone to the lengths of drugging Allan in order to have his way with him was a lot to take in. The effects of the drug had left his memory spotty over the details of that ominous date, but the corroboration of Mickey and his cousins was more than enough for him. His relationship with Thomas had taught him never to be 'less than,' despite the feelings of violation over Shakir's actions.

Allan took a long shower after hearing the events of that night. When he came out and dressed, with his mind clear, he sat down at the dining room table with his twin, Cousin Wayne, Cousin Theo, Bradley, Rico, Ronnell, and Jermaine. He had to take his power back. "I need to call Mom and Dad, and then Madear. I don't want to call the cops, but I don't want that scumbag to get away with this, either."

"Family meeting?" Cousin Wayne asked.

"Exactly." Allan grabbed his cell phone and dialed.

Michael and Lissa broke speed records getting to Minneapolis for the family meeting; nothing would have kept them from being by their son's side. Madear, upon learning of Allan's attempted rape, was outraged. With Allan's participation and consent, she made two phone calls. As a result, Shakir Delray suddenly dropped out of school, the last known whereabouts of him and his family somewhere near Barrow, Alaska.

With the encouragement and support of his family, Allan sought counseling. Over the subsequent weeks, the sessions Allan underwent aided the healing process. His parents and his twin had also given him a safe space to talk about his experience. Still, he needed more. "You know, I need to get away for a few days," he told Mickey during a study break.

Mickey put his arm around his twin in support. "I get it. Remember what we used to do when we needed time to work things out?"

"Yeah. We'd find a quiet spot on New Richmond or head over to Grand Bahama and let nature do its healing."

"Well, Minnesota has places like that. Cousin Theo and Cousin Wayne talk about the North Shore a lot."

"North Shore?"

"Yeah. According to them, it's that part of Lake Superior that borders Minnesota north of Duluth all the way up into Canada. Cousin Wayne used to go up there when he was in college at UMD."

Allan mulled it over for a few seconds. "That may be the ticket. I'll ask them."

Two days later, Allan was on the road, having driven through Duluth and now cruising up Highway 61. He found it hard to fathom that Duluth was actually a seaport or that it was also the scene of a lynching in 1920. Being the Edwards family historian, Deborah Edwards Hendricks made sure he was well-informed. For now, he was content to enjoy the drive and clear his head during this journey.

Located between Grand Marais and Grand Portage, the resort he booked offered panoramic views of Lake Superior and the nearby mountains and hills. With Mom's voice in his ears, Allan made sure to stock up on provisions and gas while in Grand Marais, even taking photos to send them. He had never crossed so many rivers on a road trip, which had him wondering, *Maybe this state should be called The Land of 10,000 Rivers.* Though he wouldn't be using it, he was grateful for cell phone reception if he needed it, as well as the ever-faithful land lines.

The cabin was clean and cozy but not claustrophobic with the basic amenities, a television, and an excellent view of the lake. He soon unpacked his things and put away the groceries, deciding to cook a meal later. After shelving his novels, he sprayed the exposed parts of his body with Cutter's, locked the door, and partook of a walk along one of the nature trails.

It took a little time for him to adjust to the absence of both city white noise and light pollution, but for his purposes, it served as an aid to still his mind. The diamond star-laden sky brought to his mind occasions he spent on remote areas of the islands, and he said a prayer of thanks for his surroundings. A good meal and a Sylvia Berry Lewis novel had his head meeting the pillow by nine p.m., sending him into a slumber he hadn't experienced in weeks.

The next day, reminiscent of times at the beach in the Bahamas, Allan was in total awe and yet calmed by the vast expanse of Lake Superior. Seated by the water, he found himself focusing on a spot out on the horizon. His breathing rate slowed, the type conducive to a meditative state. Time appeared to exist between the ticks of an unheard clock. Gradually, he witnessed a change in the place of his focus. Indistinct shapes began forming, some brown, some deep aged ivory, and one of light. *Do I need glasses?*

Allan's lips parted slightly when the shapes reached clarity. One of the shapes, to his astonishment, was himself. Behind him was a… presence. A presence of light, embracing him. Next to him, the brown features had sharpened into a man. The man appeared to be close to his age, yet his features were hidden. His own features, on the other hand, reflected gratitude, and someone deeply in love.

In that moment, he heard a voice. Not one which could be heard by physical senses, but from his spirit.

"I love you, and I'll never leave you," the voice spoke. "Keep Me first and everything will be all right. Know that you are blessed and highly favored. Before you even asked, I have already sent you your helpmate. You'll know in your heart."

The images slowly faded, and Allan experienced a peace he hadn't felt since the attempted rape. The fear and anxiety had been removed by the only one who could do it. From the family stories passed down over the years, he remembered one in particular from his Grandma Maureen when she was faced with a difficult decision concerning his Uncle Bernie. Realization set in as his eyes continued gazing out over the water. Like her, he'd had a vision, and it filled him with hope.

Chapter 8

Summer 2007

Freshman year for the Davis twins ended on a positive note academically, with both making the Dean's List. For Allan, there was gratitude for his renewed spirit. Joining them on said list were Ronnell and his boyfriend Lamar, Jermaine and his new boyfriend Marcellus, and Hari and Dylan. For their parents, this was a call for acknowledgement of jobs well done. For the young men so honored, it called for a day at Valleyfair, Minnesota's premiere amusement park.

With some effort, Allan managed to get out of his clothes and into bed that evening, full and pleasantly tired from the day's festivities. With the exception of the previous summer, idleness had never been an option for him or his twin, so he looked forward to his summer internship at Edwards Enterprises. With Cousin Douglass as CEO and Cousin Darius as CFO, they would see to it that he knew the administrative side of operating a business.

Given the events of his own life, he had given more and more thought about LGBT youth who had been kicked out of their homes. The very idea that there were parents who thought it was okay to throw their children to the wolves for their sexuality was enough to make his blood boil. It made him deeply grateful for his own extended family, as well as the parents out there who truly loved their children. *Maybe I could create a nonprofit or something.*

May gave way to June, and Allan now understood what his cousins were talking about during his first visit to Minneapolis. Temperatures were in the 80s and 90s with July forecasts of 90-plus temperatures. No wonder people flocked to the lakes in droves. At this time of year, beachgoers were a constant presence at nearby Lake Nokomis and Lake Hiawatha, and the family posse could be found swimming several times a week when they had down time.

Allan didn't begrudge his cousins or his friends the bliss of coupledom, but he had been on a dating moratorium since that chilling night with Shakir. The counseling he received helped greatly in dealing with the sense of violation, coupled with the mental and emotional exercises he applied one day at a time. Since his vision at Lake Superior, he was no longer afraid. Still, channeling his energy into his studies and work carried him but so far; after all, he was only human. On the physical side, when his dick begged him to release the tension, a bottle of lube, a towel, his hand, and privacy fit the bill, fueled by celebrity fantasies. Sure, it was only a substitute for having another man to share his passion, but this time, he was going to go about it the right way.

The 4th of July brought with it the time-honored traditions of cookouts, barbecue grills, etc., and the Hendricks-Bell household was no exception. Cousin Wayne and Cousin Theo broke out the Old School funk while everyone pitched in and did the prep work. Cousin Theo, of course, laid claim to his status as grillmaster. While he proceeded to grill the ribs, chicken, hot dogs, and burgers, Jermaine helped his dad with the potato salad, cole slaw, and baked beans. After ensuring there was plenty of ice and refreshments, the others took a rest break in anticipation of a great meal.

"Hey Cuz." Ronnell sashayed over to the patio where Allan and Mickey were relaxing.

"Hey. What's up?" Allan asked.

"Some friends of mine are having a birthday party over the weekend. Wanna come?"

"Sure."

"It's gonna be a barbecue, so dress casual."

"Are Dylan and Hari gonna to be there?"

"You know they're in London. They won't be back for a couple of weeks."

Mickey took a moment to stretch. "OK. So, who are these friends?"

"Ramsey and Roslyn Arrington. It's their birthday. Well, their birthday is actually on July 9, but since that's on a Monday, they're celebrating it July 8. Their parents know mine. You know how that goes."

They regarded each other in that quiet understanding of the "parent network." With school out, Mickey and Ronnell had been blessed with summer positions at Christopher Electronics, while Allan and Jermaine worked at Edwards Enterprises. Not that they needed the money, but their respective parents instilled certain values in them. As such, they weren't afraid of hard work.

"Where is the party gonna be?"

"At Lake Johanna in Arden Hills. It's about twenty minutes from here."

After a confirming nod, Allan replied, "Great. We're in. Now, where is the nearest fireworks show?"

"It'll be at Powderhorn Park this evening." Ronnell looked in the direction of the grill, where his father gave him the high sign. "Hey, Pops is ready. Let's get our plates."

With Sunday afternoon traffic, the drive was easy as Ronnell navigated I-35W through Minneapolis in his parents' forest green Ford Expedition and exited at County Road D, heading into Arden Hills, a small, upscale suburb of St. Paul. Given the 93-degree temperature, the air conditioning was on the maximum setting.

"Where's Lamar?" Allan asked his cousin.

"He had to do something for his dad. He's gonna get a ride out here and come back with us."

Jermaine, who was cuddled up in the back with his boyfriend, Marcellus Green, joined in. "That's probably why Daddy and Pops let us use their SUV. This way, everyone can be comfortable. Right, baby?"

Marcellus, who was an amber-complexioned version of Babyface, ran his hand across Jermaine's smooth cheek affectionately as they rounded Lake Johanna Boulevard. "Better believe it. Hey, isn't that where we're supposed to be?"

"Yeah, in the park area."

"You didn't tell them about our parents, did you?" Mickey's voice carried a note of concern.

"Don't get all paranoid on me, Cuz," was Ronnell's answer. "We know the drill."

The music was conducive to a good time, loud enough to enjoy but short of attracting complaints from local residents as they pulled into a parking space and stepped out. Most of the partygoers were gathered around the large pavilion on the north end of the lake, although some guests brought swimwear and headed over to the beach.

Allan couldn't miss the look on Mickey's face when he laid eyes on the young woman holding court at the pavilion. She was a 5'9" hotty, easily a younger version of Nia Long of *Soul Food* fame. Dressed for the heat of the day, her matching yellow top and shorts complimented and highlighted her medium brown skin, her shoulder-length black hair styled in twists. Not only that, she was curvy. Definitely his twin's type.

Mickey normally took it in stride when women threw themselves at him. Already, several young women at the party had given him flirtatious looks and sultry gazes, not to mention discreetly passing him their phone numbers before he even reached the pavilion. The object of his interest, however, wasn't doing anything—just socializing and enjoying time with her guests. He was mesmerized. "Who is *that?*" he wondered as Jermaine, Marcellus, and Ronnell approached them.

"Hey Cuzins. Let us introduce you to the guests of honor." Jermaine brought them over to the gorgeous yet unknown sistah and the young brotha standing next to her.

"Hey, birthday twins," Ronnell said brightly, giving the honorees a hug.

Jermaine followed suit with, "I'd like to introduce you to some cool dudes in our lives. Ramsey and Roslyn Arrington, these are my cousins, Mickey and Allan Davis. They're from Chicago."

Allan barely heard the introductions. His breath was stolen as he looked down and dived into Ramsey Arrington's stunning brown eyes. Standing 6'1" at 210 lbs and dressed in a Timberwolves basketball uniform, Ramsey, like his twin sister, had the looks and charm that made them among the most popular students at Mounds View High School prior to their graduation, according to his cousins. He wore his hair in a low fade and, judging from what Allan could see of his arms, chest, and legs, Ramsey kept himself in outstanding shape. As for his eyes, beautifully set in that gorgeous, medium brown face, they spoke volumes. Most important, he clearly liked what he saw in Allan. *He's checking me out. Yaassss!!*

"How do you like Minnesota?" Ramsey asked after greetings were exchanged.

"It's different, but it's been growing on us since we've been at school here." Allan hoped his friendly and casual reply would conceal his burning desire to find out if Ramsey's lips tasted as good as they looked.

"Really? Where?" Roslyn's eyes didn't leave Mickey's.

"We're at the U of M," Mickey answered in his most charming voice. "We just finished our freshman year. What about you?"

"Ramsey and I are over at Augsburg College," Roslyn answered. "High school seems like a breeze compared to college courses. Now we understand why Mama and Daddy stayed on our backs about studying and grades."

"True. It's one thing to dream and another to put in the work to achieve the dream." Ramsey gave Allan a subtle onceover, his eyes twinkling at the sight of Allan's rainbow bracelet. "You guys hungry? We can fix you a plate."

"Yeah. Those burgers look awfully good," was Allan's reply, confirmed by a nod from his twin. "And Happy Birthday to you."

When the Arrington twins turned around to prepare the plates, Allan and Mickey's mouths dropped before they took in a breath; both Roslyn and Ramsey brought meaning to the term bootylicious. They exchanged an intuitive look and immediately knew what they were going to do—get to know them and stake a claim. For Mickey, it was confirmation that the funny New Year's wish he made back in the Bahamas was coming true. For Allan, every boyfriend he ever had faded into the background in those moments. *Thomas who?*

For the duration of the birthday party, young women continued to flirt with Mickey, be it discreetly or overtly, in order to gain his attention. Mickey, however, only had eyes for Roslyn and could easily be found wherever she went. Mickey's attention toward her, to his delight, was reciprocated with the little smiles she cast in his direction.

As for Allan, he made sure he was somewhere near Ramsey, ready to talk with this hot, magnetic guy between his duties as a host and honoree. They wound up being among the last partygoers to leave, but not without Ramsey and Roslyn's numbers in their cell phones.

"Earth to Mickey, Earth to Allan, come in, come in," Jermaine teased on the drive back.

"Huh? Oh. Right." Allan felt a little embarrassed at being caught daydreaming.

"I bet I know what you're thinking about—or should I say, who," Ronnell added knowingly, giving Lamar a conspiratorial grin as they crossed the Mississippi River at downtown Minneapolis. "I saw the way you two were checking each other out."

"Okay, okay, so I think he's hot," Allan admitted. "And maybe it's a good thing he doesn't really know anything about Sunrise. Maybe that'll make it easier to…"

"Take him out on a date?" Mickey threw in.

"I see you've come back from the stratosphere, Cuz." Jermaine smirked as he gave Ronnell a high-five.

"I just know that my brother has a point. As for me…."

"Yes?"

Mickey let out a sigh of the smitten as he recalled their playful flirting at the party. "When it comes to Ms. Roslyn Arrington, I will be in full pursuit mode. But I want her to know who I am before she meets the folks."

"I know," Allan agreed. "I get this vibe from Ramsey, the vibe of a guy I'd take home to meet Mom and Dad."

Ronnell took Lamar's hand in his free one, wearing the grin of a high-priced matchmaker. "Looks like you two have it bad. Well, to ease your way and put you out of your misery, here's a little intel. From what I picked up on at the party, they're interested in you. But you'll have to step up your game. They're just like their parents. If you want to lock them down, you have to show them you're not just there to hit it and quit it. Trust and believe, they will shut that down with a quickness."

The twins breathed a sigh of relief and replied with a simultaneous, "Got it."

The very next day, after work, Allan was on his cell phone with Ramsey Arrington, wishing him official birthday greetings. Ronnell and Jermaine, of course, teased him, but he didn't care. There was something about this guy. The hell with the two-day wait before calling—in Allan's mind, Ramsey had all the early signs of a keeper, especially if Ronnell's inside intel was accurate. Besides, before he even made the call, Mickey had walked past him with his own phone, already engaged in deep conversation with Roslyn Arrington.

He had no idea where the time went as they talked and shared, but he could have listened to that baritone voice forever from the moment he heard Ramsey say, "Hey."

"Allan! Mickey! All y'all! Time for dinner!" Cousin Wayne called out.

"That's Cousin Wayne, and he holds dinner for no one. Can I call you back later?"

"Sure. I will definitely be looking forward to your call," Ramsey confirmed.

Allan's body grew warm and tingly. "Cool. Talk to you later."

All those years spent on the islands had developed Allan's love and appreciation for the outdoors, so it was a treat when Ramsey suggested a nature outing. They had only been seeing each other for a couple of weeks; their first date was at Baskin Robbins, where they dared each other to eat a LollaPalooza sundae. For this date, they were walking hand in hand along the nature trails and dunes on the Mississippi River, not far from the east bank campus of the U of M.

"Leave it to you to find a way to combine a date and a workout," Allan noted, thinking of the steep inclined sidewalk and the wooden steps they took to reach the river. "This is beautiful."

"I thought you'd like it." Ramsey squeezed his hand. "It may not be the sea or the ocean, but it has its charms."

"Do you mind if I tell you that you're part of the charm?" Allan's voice was flirtatious.

"Hey, boo. You can tell me that any time."

"Say that again. I like it."

"Like what?"

"The way you call me 'boo.'" Allan's "Beckley eyes" twinkled.

"Well, boo, there's something I've wanted to do for a bit."

"Really? And what's that?"

Ramsey gave him a sensuous smile. "Why don't we go sit by the water and you can find out?"

"I see a spot right now." Allan led Ramsey to a comfortable area just in front of the dunes. "I can hardly wait."

The brightness of the sun on that July afternoon only served to reflect the glow within Allan when Ramsey held him for that first kiss. It was gentle at first, feather kisses planted on Allan's lips. As Ramsey steadily pressed his lips against his, Allan knew he only wanted more. He wrapped his arms around Ramsey's neck, relaxing into the deepening kiss and the sensation of Ramsey's tongue meeting his. This was the kind of kiss that could go on forever as far as he was concerned. Even with guys older than he, Allan was usually the one to dominate in these situations. With Ramsey, he knew in that moment that he could enjoy being dominated as well.

The feel of Ramsey's tongue working his mouth, his hands running through his dreadlocks, was exquisitely passionate for Allan. For the first time, he was experiencing being wanted, desired, on an electrifying level. On an instinctual level, their connection held out a promise of more; for now, this was enough. The kiss was arousing in a way Allan hadn't experienced with previous boyfriends. Even before the kiss broke, his full-on erection strained at his shorts. Not that Ramsey was unaffected by the passion. Taking a glance downward, there was no mistaking the prominent outline of Ramsey's throbbing dick in his shorts. *Man, he's big.* Allan tasted Ramsey again, fighting the urge to just reach down and cup said dick. *I can work with that. But for now, I need to find out more of what's under the hood.* Even as those thoughts ran through his head, the gleam in Ramsey's eyes as they went in for more kisses told Allan that from now on, July would be his favorite month.

With all the family that was scheduled to be in town for Cousin Eli's testimonial, Allan debated whether or not to invite Ramsey, concerned that it might be overwhelming to meet so many relatives in one shot. They stayed in touch via text and cell phones on a daily basis, whether it was for a long talk or just to check in. Occasionally, they would double-date with Mickey and Roslyn. On August 1, the day before the testimonial, he sat at work, still unable to make a decision about Ramsey. Around mid-afternoon, Eli Jr. let the staff go home.

Out-of-town relatives were still arriving when Allan parked on the street near Cousin Eli's mansion. Some were chatting and relaxing across the street, enjoying Lake of the Isles. Small wonder—even in his branch of the family, it was like having a reunion. Given the valuable contributions he made to Christopher Electronics and the community over the years, Eli Edwards, Sr. richly deserved the numerous accolades he received.

Even as he was greeted by his parents and engaged in conversations with assorted relatives, Allan found himself rethinking his initial reluctance to introduce Ramsey. All his instincts about him had been positive thus far. He and Mickey had already met Ramsey and Roslyn's parents, Rodney and Lanita Arrington, who were clearly the sort of people his grandparents called "salt of the earth." What in the world was he waiting for?

Well, I might as well get it over and done with, especially since Mom and Dad are here. He pulled out his cell phone and dialed the number, only to hear a busy signal. *That's strange; Ramsey usually picks up after the second ring.* Waiting a few minutes, Allan redialed the number, receiving the drone of another busy signal.

"What's going on?" he heard his mother ask. "Every number I call is busy."

"I don't understand," Grandma Maureen said. "It's not like Allan. Unless he's in a meeting, he always picks up when I call. And I'm sure that meeting was over some time ago."

At that moment, Cousin Doris entered the room. "I just saw something on the news. I didn't want to believe it, but..."

"What?" Madear asked.

Doris' gaze locked onto the nearby television. "That."

Allan, along with his relatives, looked on in horror at the images of the collapsed I-35W bridge on the flat screen television. As the newscaster recounted the grim details, the camera panned over the wrecked cars, one of which was an eerily familiar limousine.

"Oh, God," Maureen uttered. "They're on the bridge."

He didn't need to be told who "they" were. Fear gripped him and his twin as they silently communicated the common questions. Were they all right? Were they injured? And then there was the question they were afraid to ask: did all of them survive?

With cell phone usage at a standstill, and on the verge of tears, Allan took his turn on one of the land lines and dialed a number, catching his breath when he heard a ring.

"Hello."

"Hi, Mr. Arrington, this is Allan. Is Ramsey there?"

"Yes. He just came in the door. I'll get him."

"Hey, boo," he heard Ramsey answer after a few seconds.

"Hi, bae. It's me."

"Boo, you don't sound so good. What's going on?"

Allan's voice broke. "It's about the bridge."

"I know about that. That's all we've been seeing on TV. But... wait a minute. Are you saying..."

"Yeah. My grandpa, my Aunt Vickie, my Cousin Eli…they were on it when it fell."

Ramsey heard the tears in his boyfriend's voice. "Oh, my God. What do you need me to do?"

"I'm at Uncle Eli's house right now. Could you come over?"

"Just give me the address, and I'm there. Is Mickey there?"

Allan looked across the room at his twin. "He's here. He's pretty upset."

"Don't worry. I'm bringing Roslyn with me."

The waiting became indeterminate, and the ubiquitous newscasters only served to keep everyone's nerves on edge. Grandma Maureen had asked his mother to accompany her to the hospital while his father stayed at the mansion with the bulk of family members to lend support, especially for the children there, which included Aunt Vickie's twins.

While talking with other relatives about the status of Grandpa, Aunt Vickie, and Cousin Eli, he and Mickey happened to look up and see their father and Cousin Wayne enter the family room, accompanied by Ramsey and Roslyn. The worry, the concern—it was all there in their eyes. The tears Allan had held back began to flow as he flew into Ramsey's arms. Ramsey was here, holding him, comforting him. He was here for him. With him, and with the strength of his family, Allan could get through this.

The hours since the collapse soon turned day into evening, and evening into night. During that time, Allan managed to get his emotions into enough check to introduce Ramsey to his family—as his boyfriend. "Ramsey, Roslyn, we're grateful to meet you," Michael said. "Thank you for being here for my sons."

"We wouldn't be anywhere else, Mr. Davis," Roslyn replied, gently touching Mickey's shoulder.

"Can we get you anything else?"

"Thank you, but Mrs. Carson took care of us," Ramsey said.

From the calls that did come through from the hospital, they learned that Cousin Douglass' boyfriend, Preston Welch, was also on the bridge when it collapsed. Douglass' mother, Xenobia, showed up at the hospital to make a scene, and Douglass didn't hesitate in telling her off. Madear, in turn, shut her down and sent her packing. In the meantime, everyone was on prayer watch.

Family members were camped out all over the mansion when Allan awoke the next morning with a sleeping Ramsey beside him. Gradually, the place buzzed with the activity of bathrooms being used to freshen up, breakfast prepared by Mrs. Carson and her staff, and phones that were now available for use. Mickey and Roslyn soon joined them for the morning meal, while their father engaged in a deep phone conversation.

"Any word on Grandpa and Cousin Eli? And Mr. Welch?" Mickey asked after Michael ended the call and approached them.

"Your mother says they made it through surgery, but they're still unconscious. Aunt Vickie's all right; they just want to keep her under observation."

"What about Mr. Nelson?" Allan asked.

Michael's face was grim. "He didn't make it. Cousin Debbi is staying in touch with his relatives in Waterloo."

Allan's face fell at the news of the Edwards' chauffeur's death.

Late in the afternoon, Allan and Ramsey entered the mansion after a walk by Lake of the Isles. Televisions were turned down in the immediate area of Cousin John, who was taking a call. The low volume of voices told Allan something was up, something important.

"OK…I'll tell them…bye." John ended the call and faced the expectant group. "That was Tanya. Grandpa and Cousin Allan are conscious. It'll take them a while to heal…but they're going to be all right. The same goes for Preston."

The relief over Uncle Eli and Grandpa's recovery, coupled with the comfort and support Ramsey provided during this ordeal, stirred a memory in Allan. Once again, he was back at Lake Superior, remembering the words spoken during his vision. In that moment, he knew. Ramsey Daniel Arrington was The One. And Allan also knew what he wanted to do.

Together with Mickey, Allan took Ramsey and Roslyn over to their parents. "I know you've already been introduced to our parents, but there's something else about them you need to know," Allan spoke from trust. "They're part of Sunrise."

Chapter 9

Fall 2008

Despite the peer pressure surrounding them, Allan and Ramsey stayed on their course of truly getting to know each other over the next year via dating, sharing interests and goals, and soul-searching conversations. These days, matchmaker guru Patti Stanger would call what they were doing "looking under the hood." During this process, the sexual chemistry was ever present, from which they became most creative with hand jobs, blow jobs, and plenty of making out. However, for their own respective reasons, they refrained from going all the way. Mickey and Roslyn were no different. There was no question that Roslyn Arrington was the right woman for his twin. The fact that she made him wait served as confirmation in Allan's mind.

Labor Day weekend of 2008 brought both families together again at Lissa and Michael's beautiful home. The beaches along Chicago's lakefront were pretty full, with people anxious to take advantage of the last holiday before fall set in. While their parents relaxed and enjoyed each other's company, along with other Christopher relatives that stopped in, Allan, Mickey, Ramsey, and Roslyn took off for the dunes on the North Shore up in Lake County.

While Michael, Rodney Arrington, and Travis Mitchell discussed the latest musicians and baseball over the barbecue grill, Lissa and Lanita Arrington, along with Vickie and Ms. Bond, were in the kitchen finishing the prep work for the cookout. They had enjoyed an evening out on the town that Saturday with their husbands, and now they were ready for their afternoon meal, followed by a visit to Lissa and Vickie's parents at their estate in Evanston later on.

"Just you wait, Vickie. Your kids will be grown and tying the knot before you know it," Lissa playfully teased her sister.

"Please. They're only 12," Vickie groaned, thinking of her twins.

"Oh, that's right. Fasten your seat belts; the teenage years are upon you." Lanita gave Vickie a knowing smirk. "You're in for a wild ride. All we did was blink, and now our kids are in college."

"And from all the evidence, it's a sure bet there will be wedding bells sometime in their future. Hopefully after they graduate." Lissa gave Lanita a high-five.

Lanita savored the thought. "Don't you just love it, Lissa? Twins marrying twins."

"Not to mention the grandchildren we'll get," Lissa replied with an infectious grin.

"Do you think our grandchildren will come in twin sets?"

Lissa thought for a moment. "Well, in my family, it skips a generation. Mama's a twin; her brother, my Uncle Mitch who lives in Brooklyn. But the closest she came with the eight of us were Irish twins."

"Irish twins?"

"Yes. Champ, Tanya, and I were all born less than a year apart," Vickie added. "Then Josh, Champ, Lissa, and I have twins, while Marty outdid everybody with sextuplets. No question, multiple births run in our family. What about yours, Lanita?"

Lanita beamed, her rich brown skin glowing. "In mine, every generation has at least one set of twins. My brothers, Lloyd and Lyle, are twins. Lloyd has a son, but Lyle has twin daughters. And I have Ramsey and Roslyn."

"I'd say the odds have just been increased dramatically," Lissa concluded as she and Lanita relished the prospects.

"And remember what Mama says about having grandchildren," Vickie stated. "After you get done playing with them and spoiling them, you can send them back to their parents. I should know, now that Mama's doing that with Travis and Traci."

"What has she planned this time?"

"She's taking them and a couple of their friends to Marriott's Great America after church. You know how spry she is."

"Is Father going?"

"Are you kidding? Try and stop him."

"Can you believe it? Three more weeks and it's back to school." Ramsey squeezed Allan's hand while they relaxed on a beach blanket in the dunes, watching Mickey and Roslyn cavorting in Lake Michigan along with other couples and families.

"I know. But it's been fun. And just think…"

"Yeah. We get to vote in the presidential election this time."

"True. Grandpa, Cousin Eli, and Madear have gone all out on the fundraisers. I'm sure Obama will be the talk of Madear's fall party. And guess what?"

"What?"

"E. Lynn Harris is going to be her special guest."

"Cool. Mama will love that. He's one of her favorite authors. She has all his books."

"Well, she's in good company. Cousin John and Cousin Sylvia will probably be there with books in hand for an autograph." Allan's eyes turned flirty. "You know, I was thinking…"

"What?"

"Since we have the opportunity, let's go away somewhere next weekend. Just the two of us. Somewhere that no one would even think of looking for us."

"I'm all for that, boo. Anything special on the agenda?" Ramsey's voice was provocative.

"You, bae." Allan caressed Ramsey's pecs and tweaked a nipple. "And me." He discreetly slid his hand down to his boyfriend's crotch and squeezed. "And taking things to the next level. While we're away, I want you to fuck me."

"Mmmmmm. I *love* the way you think," Ramsey purred in delight, his dick hardening in his swim trunks as he pulled Allan in for a promising kiss.

Allan was thankful that he filed away Wisconsin Dells in his memory. Given the height of the season and the type of crowds that visited the area, it was the last place anyone would look for them. A 10-minute drive from Lake Delton, the moderately priced business suite was perfect for their purposes. No doubt, he and Ramsey would take full advantage of the water-themed parks—by day, that is. By night, well…

They barely got inside the suite before Ramsey was on his boyfriend, kissing him while reaching inside his damp swim trunks. Allan moved to wrap his arms around Ramsey, but Ramsey was too quick, already on his knees and yanking down Allan's trunks in one fell swoop, freeing Allan's achingly hard dick.

"Oh, fuck," Allan groaned, wrapped up in the warm wetness of Ramsey's mouth. They had been on the edge of anticipation since they left one of the water parks, wrapping beach towels around themselves so people wouldn't notice the dick prints in their trunks. Even then, Ramsey had dared Allan to take his dick out in the SUV while he squeezed it. In fact, Ramsey made it harder to concentrate on driving by pulling out his own dick and stroking it.

He knew he wouldn't last long. Perhaps it would take a little of the edge off for when Ramsey put all that dick of his inside him; goodness knows he had a short recovery time when it came to sex. In a fog of pleasure, he looked down into Ramsey's eyes as Ramsey deep-throated him with a hunger. In the frenzy of desire, Ramsey had slipped off his own trunks and was stroking his thick, hot dick with his free hand.

The sight of Ramsey and the feelings from his expert ministrations were too much for Allan. He cried out, holding Ramsey's head while shooting a load of jizz down his throat, barely able to stand against the door. To his credit, Ramsey swallowed most of it, with the exception of some rivulets that ran down his chin. Standing up, eyes filled with love and desire, Ramsey leaned into Allan for a passionate kiss.

Allan loved that slightly zoned-out feeling he experienced after coming in Ramsey's mouth. Kissing his boyfriend while tasting himself on his lips was heady. His dick was still achingly erect.

And yet…that siren call, the one that occupied his mind for months, wanted more. Breaking the kiss, Allan's eyes expressed the need that would no longer wait.

"Bae?" he asked huskily as Ramsey caressed his plump, round, phat ass.

Ramsey's voice dropped to the sensual register. "What is it, boo?"

"I'm so ready. I want it."

"What is it you want?" It was only a question, but Ramsey's inflections made it passionately naughty.

"I want you to fuck me. Now. I want to feel you inside me. I want it so bad."

Ramsey's dick throbbed with increased desire at the sound of Allan's plea. "How bad do you want it, boo?"

"Real bad, bae. Real bad." Allan's eyes lowered to the hardness of Ramsey's beautiful brown dick, his breathing deepening.

Ramsey believed his boyfriend from the way he shuddered with pleasure when he put a finger between his aged-ivory cheeks, rubbing it over his hole. "Then you've got it, 'cause I've wanted you since forever."

They reached the king-sized bed faster than one could say "Afro Mystic." While Ramsey opened the drawer in the nightstand to retrieve the bottle of lube, Allan lay back on the bed stroking himself, feasting his eyes on the hot, thoroughly aroused man before him. Ramsey's hot dick was nearly as big as his, and he had enjoyed stroking it, taking him in his mouth. Though Allan had topped guys, he had never bottomed before. Ramsey was about to change all that, and he could hardly wait. The fact they had been tested six months ago and the results were negative paved the way for even greater intimacy.

He felt his anal walls clench but only for a couple of seconds before opening up and accepting Ramsey's lubed, sensuous fingers. They slowly stroked inside of him, making Allan squirm with pleasure and desire for more. All too soon, mere fingers were insufficient. He wanted Ramsey thrusting deep inside him, taking him, claiming him. "Please, bae. Please *fuck* me," he begged in a voice heavy laden with want and need.

Ramsey's shaft was leaking pre-cum, his breathing heavier. He drank in the sight of Allan laid out on the king-sized bed, holding his long, muscular legs up, his brown hole twitching and puckering, "Beckley eyes" glazed over with need. Knowing that he had caused those sensations, that he would be the first—and if he had his wish, the *only*—man to be inside Allan had Ramsey beyond ready. *How did I ever get so lucky to have this man?* Lining his dick up to Allan's hole, he slowly entered him, sealing the entry with a kiss when he was balls deep inside him. *Whoa. My boo was truly worth the wait.*

The sensations of being filled up by Ramsey sent Allan into an ecstasy he had never known before. "Yeah, oh yeah. Fuck me, bae," he moaned as his boyfriend began a slow, rhythmic motion with his hips that stroked his P-spot. His big, thick rod was hard as a diamond, throbbing from the pleasure he felt from inside, the intense connection he and Ramsey shared in those moments. Previous boyfriends couldn't hold a match to Ramsey in any area, not even Thomas. Joined as one, their connection was beyond amazing. At that moment Ramsey's shaft hit his P-spot again, urging even more passionate moans from him.

He loved the desire spread across Ramsey's face as their eyes locked onto each other, knowing that look was for him—and only him. Raising his head, Allan was rewarded with a smoldering kiss that served to arouse him further. *Oh, you're so big, and you feel so good.* He wrapped his long legs around Ramsey's waist, pushing his booty back at him to take his dick deeper, savoring the erotic dance they were enfolded in.

As waves of pleasure washed over the couple, Ramsey's strokes became deeper and gained momentum. Allan, gasping from the sexual intensity, squeezed his walls around his boyfriend while he gazed rapturously at him, drawing moans of endearment from Ramsey, wanting to draw out their lovemaking as long as possible, and he wasn't disappointed. Allan didn't know whether minutes or hours had passed; he was so lost in their passion, he didn't care. It built and built and built until Ramsey made one final deep stroke, hitting his special spot with surefire accuracy. Feeling the warm jets of release filling him and the heartfelt cry of climax, Allan's own orgasm crashed over him in shouts of ecstasy, bolts of semen coating their chests.

Allan awoke sated and happy in Ramsey's arms the next morning, gently extricating himself to make breakfast. His ass twitched at the memory of the multiple times Ramsey fucked him last night, putting yet another grin on Allan's face. *Someone's been talking to Mom,* he deduced at the sight of the earplugs Ramsey wore. *I'll bet Mom had a talk with Roslyn, too.* He had never considered his snoring as loud—loud was something reserved for his great-uncle, Theo Davis. Well, it was all relative, and if it took earplugs to keep Ramsey happy, sobeit.

Drawing on his own tips from Mom and Ms. Bond, Allan walked over to the kitchen area of their suite, gathering the groceries they purchased to make his special omelets along with toast, grits, sausage, and hash browns to complement the meal. He was grateful they had taught him and his brother how to cook, for this would be the first of many meals he would gladly make for his man.

He had just finished setting the table, gracing it with two full glasses of orange juice, when he heard movement behind him. Looking back, he beheld the hotness of Ramsey dressed only in a pair of basketball shorts, his dick print pleasingly visible. The tingly, wonderful feeling in Allan's body took over as he gave his boyfriend a Pepsodent smile coupled with a meaningful look from his "Beckley eyes."

"Good morning, boo." Ramsey's voice possessed a sleepy but well-loved tone to it. "You never told me you could cook. I love it."

"One of my hidden talents." Allan pulled out a chair for Ramsey after he kissed him. "As Mom has often said, 'a man must have sustenance,' and you are one hot, amazing man."

"Careful, boo," Ramsey teased, "or you'll have me bending you over that table."

"I hope you do, bae." Allan watched Ramsey's shorts begin to tent, giving him a sexy smirk while his own dick thickened at the prospects. "But first, we need to eat. *Then,* we can fuck like rabbits."

Upon his return to Minneapolis a few days later, Allan and Mickey met on the basketball court. One look at Mickey was all it took; not only did his brother get lucky, he was over the moon. Small wonder—Allan knew he gave off the same energy.

His body still tingled from the *tour de force* of Ramsey's lovemaking the night before, kissing him, sucking him, pounding into him, claiming him again. Yes, being made love to by Ramsey Arrington was, beyond all doubt, something he had taken to like a canvasback to water.

"That good, huh?" Mickey wore a knowing smirk.

"Takes one to know one," Allan returned with the smile of a satisfied man. "When it's the one you love, it's mind-blowing. And your lovely Roslyn knows you, too."

"Better believe it. She is someone I'd have a song written for. Know anybody that can do it?"

Allan sunk a three-pointer and paused, pretending to think it over. "Well…yeah. Right after I write one for Ramsey."

"Cool," Mickey beamed, going in for a brotha hug as the other members of the team began to enter the gym.

That night, Allan entered his dorm room after a refreshing shower, smelling of his favorite body wash and drying his dreadlocks. His jaw dropped in pleasant awe and delight at the sight of a naked Ramsey, twerking his bootylicious butt at him to the tune of their favorite house music. With a naughty grin, Ramsey spread his luscious, medium brown cheeks, giving Allan a serious eyeful of his winking hole. "Boo, I can hardly describe what it's like being inside you. So hot, so tight, so wet, like you were made for me. That's somewhere I want to be again and again."

Allan gave him a throaty growl. "You'd better believe I want you to."

"Yeah. But now, before I have to go in the morning, I want to feel all that dick of yours up in me." Hard as a rock, he gazed pointedly at Allan's steadily rising erection separating the towel before he met his sultry "Beckley eyes." "This ass is all yours, boo. I want you to fuck me senseless."

Allan did not have to be told twice. With a quick swab of lube, Ramsey soon lowered himself on Allan's dick, riding it like he was born in the saddle, and Allan loved every tantalizing, sizzling, exquisitely wonderful moment of it. Talk about off the charts! Being inside Ramsey, and having Ramsey inside him, joined by the love and passion they had for each other, was truly one of life's great pleasures. Allan gasped in rapture as Ramsey raised and lowered himself for maximum pleasure while his big butt jiggled in response. He was thrilled at the sight of Ramsey stroking his own throbbing dick, leaking a steady stream of pre-cum, coupled with his moans of unparalleled bliss.

Even as he was caught up in the happiness of the moment, Allan relished the thought of them giving this kind of pleasure to each other regularly, if the sensations in his own booty were any indication. He sat up to kiss Ramsey, and a switch flipped that sent them into hyperspace.

"I…I…" Ramsey came like Old Faithful, clenching his muscles around Allan's pleasure-inducing dick, coating his face and their chests with his release, spurring Allan into an orgasm that left the gravity pull. As he filled Ramsey's depths, his heart filled with the love he had for his man, savoring the moments of sublime bliss.

After that, the floodgates were open. During that first month, aside from classes, their friends and family saw less of the couple, lost as they were in the torrid passion of lovemaking. As far as Allan was concerned, Ramsey Arrington had thoroughly ruined him for any other man. The way he wanted Ramsey, and how Ramsey passionately wanted him, only made Allan fall deeper in love with him.

At times when he was studying at Wilson Library, he found himself daydreaming of Ramsey's sensuous kisses and the fullness of his majestic dick thrusting inside him. His inner walls would clench with desire while his penis throbbed with arousal, preventing him from getting up from his study carrel too soon. Sometimes, he'd overhear other gay and bi guys on campus writing off men like him being "strict tops" who would never bend over or lift their legs for another man. Allan often wore a smug smirk on his face during those occasions. *If only you knew. All it takes is the right conditions, the right chemistry, with the right guy. Ramsey can fuck me anytime he wants to, and he knows how much I love it. Yes, I'll take his dick every chance I can get it. I'm so glad Uncle Sammy told me there was no such thing as a "strict top," only guys who are very picky about who they bottom for.*

Though dorm rooms were all right, having their own space off campus was better. With the help of family friend Deshawna Berry Randolph, Allan and Ramsey found a comfortable two-bedroom apartment near Minnehaha Park and set up housekeeping in early October. Mickey and Roslyn, also with her help, moved into an apartment with comparable amenities across the river in the Highland Park neighborhood of St. Paul. Allan already knew that, with the exception of certain areas, Roslyn would have a major influence in decorating their apartment, and Mickey would wisely let her have her head. The same held true for Ramsey, although Allan had ideas that blended in well with the overall result. In the end, they created an environment that was both pleasing to the eye yet comfortable for living space.

Their junior year of college started off with more challenges in their respective majors, and with it, more papers to write and extra study time. Now that they were living together, Allan noticed how driven Ramsey was when it came to his schoolwork. He was also more irritable during midterms when the amount of papers he was required to write became increasingly demanding. Although homework came easy to Allan—his mother said he took after his Uncle M&M—Ramsey had to work harder to get the grades he desired. Sometimes, he wouldn't eat properly when burning the midnight oil, and Allan would quietly leave him a snack and tend to his own assignments.

“Boo, I know I’ve been a grouch lately, and I’m sorry,” Ramsey said after he came home from taking midterm exams one evening.

“Hey. I get it, bae. You have to stop being so hard on yourself.” Allan wrapped his arms around him in a caring embrace. “Is there anything I can do to help?”

“I don’t know how you put up with me sometimes. You’ve been a big help in making sure I eat and all. But there is one thing you can do to help relieve the tension right now.”

“And what is that?”

Ramsey’s eyes grew sultry and filled with need. “I need you to fuck me. I need to feel you working my ass. I love the way you kiss me while you’re inside me. Boo, you know how to do it.”

Allan, his dick hardening in his shorts from that baritone-voiced plea, gave his boyfriend a naughty grin. Unzipping Ramsey’s jeans, he reached inside the waistband of his boxer briefs, sensuously squeezing Ramsey’s gorgeous phat butt before he fingered his hole. Ramsey moaned in delight. “We aim to please, bae.”

And he did—thoroughly. Hours later, Ramsey lay curled up against him like a relaxed, contented feline, basking in afterglow. “I love you, boo. I so needed that.”

Allan caressed Ramsey’s shoulders, softly kissing the back of his neck. “I love you too, bae.”

Chapter 10

Spring 2010

"Are you up for a trip?" Allan asked during their senior year as he and Ramsey walked across the Macalester College campus to meet up with Ronnell, Lamar, Dylan, and Hari.

"I'm always up for that—soon as I finish my assignments. Where?"

"Los Angeles."

"And what's the occasion?"

"Well…Dad's been nominated for an Oscar."

Ramsey's jaw dropped. "No."

"Yes. We've been out there for the Grammys before, but we've always gone solo. This time, I want you there with me. And in case you're wondering, Mickey's asking Roslyn as we speak."

"Try and keep me away, boo," Ramsey chuckled. "I will Velcro myself to you."

Allan squeezed his hand in delight. "Good answer, bae. Good answer."

Meeting up on campus the next day, Allan and Mickey happily discussed their plans for the upcoming trip to Los Angeles, excited about actually having a plus-one to bring to the awards ceremonies. They and Ramsey had opted for custom made, classic black tuxedos. Roslyn, of course, took the invitation as a golden opportunity to shop for a gown with the right amount of glitz to walk down a red carpet, plus accessories. "After all, Arringtons must represent," was her response.

Knowing they would never be forgiven if they didn't spend time at the ranch during their visit, Lissa made a call to Uncle Sammy and Uncle Darnell to expect them after the awards show. Her younger brother Bernie, now living on the ranch with his family, could also be counted upon for comment if they didn't stop by. "Now you know you can take more than a few days to unwind here after all the craziness in L.A.," Sammy declared.

"Your point is well taken, Uncle Sammy, and we are going to take you up on your offer," Lissa replied. "How are Bernie and his family doing?"

"They're great, and they'll be glad to see you."

"After being city people all their lives, they seem to have adjusted to ranch life pretty well."

"That was our biggest concern when we presented our offer to him, Allison. But Bernie surprised us, and we couldn't be happier to have them here to carry on our legacy."

"I know. That being said, you'll have our itinerary in a week. We're looking forward to seeing you, Uncle Sammy."

"Likewise, Allison. Likewise."

Red carpet events were nothing new to Allan and Mickey, given that Sunrise was the recipient of multiple Grammys, an NAACP Image Award, and other awards during the ensemble's long career. This time around, their father and Ronnell Hayes had composed an original music score for a movie, one that earned them an Oscar nomination. As such, the entire Sunrise family was in attendance for the Academy Awards ceremony, only this time their party included Ramsey and Roslyn. There had been the usual number of reporters and paparazzi around when Sunrise did press conferences and concerts in Chicago and other cities since their return to the U.S., as well as for the causes that were near and dear to them. Since they were new to this level of scrutiny, Ramsey and Roslyn deeply appreciated the coaching Michael and Lissa gave them prior to the event.

"From the time we leave this limo, we're going to be on," Michael said calmly. "Just smile, hold your head up, and be yourselves.

Confidence is everything. The focus will be mainly on Ronnell and me. We'll answer a few questions, but not too many. We shake some hands and keep it moving. In the event we win, they'll want us for a photo op."

"You know they'll probably have questions about Ramsey and me," Allan observed.

"Probably, since they'll be speculating about both you and Mickey. This appearance will lay that to rest. It won't be that much different from the interview we did before we left the Bahamas," Lissa replied. "Allan, you have Ramsey. Mickey, you have Roslyn. Ramsey, Roslyn, you have our sons' backs, and we have yours. So what if they ask? We're proud of you. Anyone with eyes will see how much you love each other."

Michael nodded in agreement with his wife. "And we're controlling the contact. Whether Sunrise wins or not, we will certainly give them something to talk about."

"We sure will," Mickey declared. "Let's do it."

The three couples made a dazzling walk down the red carpet to the Kodak Theater, holding hands and smiling confidently to the flash of cameras and reporters wanting sound bites. This wasn't the first time that musicians and recording artists had been nominated in this category, so they hoped this night would place them in the ranks with Isaac Hayes and Prince as Oscar winners.

They worked the crowd as they headed into the auditorium in keeping with their tradition for these events—not too early, but not too late. Sol, Medford, and their families were already in the assigned seating for Sunrise when they arrived, as were Ronnell and Jalani.

The Academy Awards show, being what it is, carried a level of cautious anticipation among the nominees, even as the cameras and commentators focused on who was present, candid moments, and of course, fashion commentary. As Oscars were awarded to the various winners, Allan and Mickey did their best to relax, bolstered by touches of endearment from Ramsey and Roslyn.

Midway through the program, the presenters took the stage to announce the nominees in the category of Best Original Music Score.

Jalani squeezed Ronnell's hand in support, while Michael held Lissa's hands in his own. The well-groomed Price Waterhouse representative walked onstage with the results, handing them to the presenters as though they held the combination to Fort Knox. The entire Sunrise party held hands in a silent prayer…

"And the winners are…"

I love you, and I will never leave you, Allan heard in his mind…

"Michael Davis and Ronnell Hayes."

Celebration abounded in the Sunrise party, surrounded by the applause from the audience. Allan beamed with pride as he watched his father and Ronnell walk up to the stage to accept their awards, the theme song they created providing the backdrop for their victory.

During his acceptance speech, Michael, as always, was thrilled yet humble as he gave his thanks to God and the people who made the award possible, including, of course, his mother, his family, and the Sunrise family. As he did so, the cameras panned back and forth to his family. His love-filled eyes scanned the audience until they rested on Lissa, touching her heart when he said, "Lissa Davis, my amazing, incredible, beautiful wife, I want to thank you for all your love and support these past 26 years. You're my 'Afro-Mystic' lady, now and forever."

Ronnell, after giving his acceptance kudos, concluded with, "And I want to give thanks to my Sunrise family, and especially the love of my life, Jalani Austin. You've been right there by my side through the most important times of my life, first as my friend, then as my partner. I love you, babe. We made it." Looking down the row, Allan saw Jalani, a tear running down his cheek and a heartwarming grin on his face, with eyes only for Ronnell. Pulling Ramsey in for another hug and kiss as his father and Ronnell left the stage with Oscars in hand, Allan continued to bask in the joy and happiness of the moment.

Once the Sunrise party stepped out of their limos, the celebration at the ranch was on with Uncle Sammy and Uncle Darnell leading the pack. Family and ranch hands alike greeted them with whoops, cheers, back slaps, handshakes, hugs, and a Skype call from Grandpa

Allan, Grandma Maureen, and Grandma Saralynne Davis. A huge "Congratulations Sunrise" sign hung over the hall of the main house. Indeed, though it was exciting to receive the Oscar onstage, this celebration meant far more.

Upon their return to school after the Academy Awards show, the twins weren't surprised by the attention they received from people who, up until then, had only talked to them casually. On the basketball court in the gym, their teammates were good-natured in their comments and teasing. A reporter from *The Minnesota Daily* approached them for a story, now that their father's Oscar win placed them squarely on the radar.

When asked about their own aspirations, Mickey replied, "I'm looking forward to being part of Sunrise. Of course, Mom and Dad will expect no less from me than they do the rest of Sunrise, which means paying my dues. That's one thing about this business. Being their son will get my foot in the door; the difference is, I have to prove myself in ways others don't. But it is what it is, and I'm OK with that."

"And what about you, Allan? Any plans for a musical career?" the reporter asked.

"I like to write songs, but it's more of a hobby. I want to add my voice and my position to help LGBT youth. There are still kids out there who aren't protected and loved the way I am. It's 2010, and many are still kicked out of their homes because of who they love. And if you're LGBT and a person of color, it's harder." Allan put his arm around Mickey. "My brother, like my parents, has always supported me. I'm firmly behind him to represent a new generation of Sunrise. He supports me in doing what I can to create safe spaces for those who need it. And we're extremely proud of what Mom and Dad and the Sunrise family have accomplished."

Okeidi, of course, was beside herself; an Academy Award win put her favorite clients in greater demand. Already, she had received offers for Michael and Ronnell to compose and arrange musical scores for three movies and to provide the musical talent, not to mention the increased sales for Sunrise's music. "I remember the first time you came to my office," she told Lissa over lunch at the Oakbrook Terrace Mall a couple of weeks later. "When I heard your demo tape, I knew I was listening to real talent, from the instrumentals to your voice. And your voice, Lissa…only God could give you a gift like that."

"Yes, He did," Lissa agreed. "Mother says she knew when I was a little girl, and she's always supported me. Now look where we are."

"Yes, indeed. 28 years, and Sunrise is still going strong!"

"Amen."

"By the way, did you find a place for it?"

"Michael didn't waste any time getting it situated when we got home. It has its own spot in the study along with the Grammys and the other awards."

"Now why am I not surprised?"

"Tell me about it. As for Father…well, there's no stopping him from bragging on us. Remember how he insisted on having a victory party as soon as we landed in Chicago?"

"I do. That party was a blowout." Okeidi reminisced over the celebration, filled with family and all the Who's Who of Chicago. When Allan Beckley Christopher hosted a party, attendance was guaranteed. "Next to your mother, he's become your biggest champion. He's come a long way from the man who told you to 'get a real job.'"

"Don't I know it. And soon my sons will graduate with their degrees. This commencement means even more than the last one."

"I know that's right, Lissa. This time, they're free to be themselves, especially Allan."

Not long after Sunrise's Oscar win, Allan's notoriety as a son of music legends reminded him that 'normal' was somewhat different for him, and it accosted him in the form of Aiden Kirkland, III. Allan had noticed Aiden in passing during his senior year, and they shared a business class together during second semester. Aiden was the poster boy for a white gay jock, supposedly the top of the gay dating food chain—6'0", blond hair, blue eyes, chiseled body, etc. Prior to confirmation of his identity, Allan was at least on friendly speaking terms with his classmates. Aiden, however, hardly gave him the time of day.

Now, Aiden was all up in his face, slathering on the charm, wanting to be friends. Allan, of course, was leery. His experience with Shakir had fine-tuned his senses when it came to spotting a predator, and for all the veneer, he knew Aiden was one of them. When Aiden made his move one day after class, Allan was quick with a flat-out, "No, thanks. I've got a man."

"What's that have to do with anything, Al? I'm just out for a little fun." Aiden's eyes lowered, zooming in on Allan's jean-covered crotch. "And from what I can see, you've got the equipment to handle some fun. Hey, nobody has to know but us."

Having been around Madear for the past four years, Allan gave the spoiled white guy his version of The Look. Staring Aiden down from his full height of 6'5", his voice temperature dropped to -20 degrees. "Unless you want more than your feelings hurt, get out of my face. Now."

Aiden, sensing that Allan was more than ready to carry out his threat, backed off in frustration. Allan headed in the opposite direction, knowing the jock would be trouble. Aiden's expression and attitude were that of someone who wasn't used to people saying no to him, and Allan shared his concerns with Ramsey at home later that day.

"I don't know what it is, bae, but that guy hasn't given up. He's going to find some way to create a problem."

"Whatever it is, boo, I've got your back. The whole family does. Now, what do you know about this douchebag?"

"Only that he transferred here this year. The way he dresses says upper-middle-class WASP, like in that old movie *Ordinary People.*"

"And now he wants you. You know what I think?"

"I bet we're thinking the same thing."

"I think he's one of those celebrity fuckers. He's never paid you any attention before…"

"And now that he knows who I am, he'll do whatever it takes to get me as a notch on his belt. That way, he can say he fucked a celebrity and have his white-boy fantasy all in one."

"Sounds like this guy's used to having men fall at his feet."

"Yeah. And I'm the one who shut him down. You can bet he's not taking that well."

"You know, boo, it's times like these when I wish we attended the same college."

"In any case, bae, watch your back. If he checked out the awards show on YouTube, he may know who you are as well. We need to find out more."

Indeed, a week later a blurb from a tabloid told an unflattering tale about Ramsey being a paid escort at the time he met Allan, including a candid photo of the two of them at the Academy Awards show. Mysteriously, the blurb spread its poisonous way across campus and other outlets. That same day, Aiden was lurking about, making another play for Allan, which was promptly rejected. *No one disses my bae and gets away with it,* Allan growled after reading the filth. *It's time to do some digging, and I know just the people who can help us.*

"Now, one of the keys to handling this is to keep from giving this salacious story any more energy while we handle the jerk responsible for this," Okeidi said during the family meeting at the Edwards mansion, which included Sunrise. She indicated Rodney and Lanita Arrington. "It's hard when you have reporters and paparazzi prowling around your door, especially when your children are the targets. But you know the saying: 'When there's no audience, the show's over.'"

"Tell me about it," Rodney Arrington scoffed. "We've become experts with the phrase, 'No comment.' Somebody there barely passed Creative Writing 101."

Okeidi's expression was empathetic. "I know, Rodney. This is a downside of the business. I'm just glad people didn't find out about Mickey and Allan being here before now."

"Well, we know who's behind it," Allan stated emphatically. "I saw right through his fake sympathy."

"Yeah. I wanted to beat the crap out of him when I found out about the story, but that would only play into his hands," Ramsey added. "What have you found out?"

Madear pulled out her dossier. "To start with, Aiden Kirkland, III attended three colleges before he came to the U of M. He's a piece of work with an overblown sense of entitlement and white privilege. He stirs up trouble and then does a 'cut and run' before he's held accountable for his actions. It's rare that people say no to him, but when they do, he becomes a brat worthy of Veda in *'Mildred Pierce.'"* The older adults nodded in recognition of the movie reference. "He's bright, but not that bright, and we were able to follow the trail to him. Beneath those all-American looks, he's the biggest manwhore in town, and Little Allan is the one that got away."

"In short, Aiden wanted to break them up by ruining my son's reputation. That way, he thought he could get Allan for himself." Lanita's face was grim, and Lissa empathized with her, as did the rest of the Sunrise ensemble.

"Exactly, Lanita. As for his parents, they live an upper-middle-class, gated community life thanks to the family business, but now that business is in serious trouble. Aiden Kirkland, Jr. made some bad investments and has taken out substantial business loans. Their house is mortgaged to the hilt. Aiden III, according to my sources, is either unaware or in denial of his family's financial trouble. He's only concerned about getting what he wants." She passed the dossier to Grandpa Allan.

"Fascinating reading," Grandpa Allan noted when he reached certain passages.

"It sounds like we have a strategy," Michael Davis concurred, steepling his fingers.

"Indeed we do. Allison, Michael, Okeidi, you handle the publicity side. Donna, Rodney, Lanita, and I will handle the private side." Grandpa Allan turned to Little Allan and Ramsey, who sat with hopeful expressions. "We've got you."

With lightning speed, the Kirklands received a visit from the IRS, demanding an audit of the past five years. Allan Beckley Christopher bought their loans, and the business folded; fortunately, Allan brought its best employees into Christopher Electronics. Their pristine suburban home went into foreclosure. Not only was Aiden

III's sports car repossessed, he was forced to work at a McDonald's. He was expelled from school when it came to light that his school papers were written by others and his exam results were bought. His last sighting was in Miami, working in the very profession he used to smear Ramsey Arrington with.

They didn't stop there. The tabloid that printed the hateful fiction about Ramsey was purchased in trust. Under new management, the sleaze element was cleaned out, and in its place was born a community newspaper worthy of the best of the Black press. Allan Beckley Christopher and Madear smiled in satisfaction. All it took were two phone calls. They always protected what was theirs.

On Commencement Day of 2010, a strong showing of Christophers, Edwardses, and related friends attended the graduation ceremonies for their beloved twins. They may not have graduated summa cum laude like their Uncle M&M, but their magna cum laude status was more than acceptable. With the help of Ronnell Hendricks-Bell and Bradley Edwards, Allan created a rainbow tassel to accessorize his cap and gown, a symbol of the freedom he never fully experienced as a high school student. And of course, Ramsey and Roslyn were in attendance, firmly standing behind their men.

This time around, Michael and Lissa were free to express their pride in their sons, and they didn't care who was around them. In fact, their respective parents fervently shared in the cheers when the twins strutted up to receive their diplomas; having Allan Beckley Christopher, Dr. Maureen Moore Christopher, and Saralynne Davis in attendance was noteworthy. Not only that, Allan and Mickey shared a joy in spirit that radiated from them, young adults ready to make their mark in the world.

Chapter 11

Summer 2010

Having finished his latest call with Little Allan and Ramsey, Sammy stepped into the bedroom to undress and prepare for bed. Darnell had turned in an hour earlier, what with a time-consuming day at the ranch and a business meeting with their nephew Sherman. Of course, Iris' hearty meals were also a contributing factor, something appreciated by all the ranch hands. As for himself, having Bernie there to take over the majority of the veterinary responsibilities had been a godsend. With established offices in Victorville and San Bernardino, Sammy's nephew soon became one of the go-to vets in the area, especially during the foaling season.

He was also grateful that Bernie and Sherman's children—Jesse, Bruce, and his namesake Sam—had fallen in love with the ranch, working side by side with the ranch hands. Sam, as it was, loved to follow him around the place, always ready and willing to help take care of the animals. *Dare I hope that Sam will follow in the family tradition?*

After 16 years, Sammy still liked to watch Darnell sleep sometimes, although he'd never let his husband know it. There was a peace about him, knowing their ranch was in good hands. If they weren't spooning, Darnell usually slept on his right side with one arm under the pillow, as he was now. Sammy finished putting on his lightweight pajamas, his eyes resting on Darnell's work-toughened right hand. In that moment, his heart and his mind were filled with memories of a special night:

Memorial Day 2008 found the couple in Hawaii on a getaway vacation. They loved sightseeing, the first stop being the USS Arizona memorial at Pearl Harbor. It was easy for them to spot other World War II vets there with their families, and Sammy and Darnell soon found themselves sharing their stories with the other vets, the common bond of a wartime nation 60-odd years ago.

A day of sightseeing brought them back to their hotel suite for a nap. As the owners of a working ranch, it was rare that they dressed for dinner unless they were eating out with a client, but Darnell had insisted upon it when they woke up. Darnell still cut a dashing figure in his custom tailored, navy blue suit with his dress Stetson and boots, and Sammy ate up the way his man checked him out, dressed in his white dinner jacket and black dress slacks, saying, "Mmmm, mmmm, mmm."

The hotel's five-star restaurant was blessed by the panoramic backdrop of the Pacific Ocean. Their table, graced with a red rose and placed in a semi-private location, gave it an air of romance and intimacy. Sammy's curiosity was piqued. From the glint in his eyes, he suspected that Darnell's plans commemorated the day they met. Wisely, Sammy sat back to enjoy the meal and the ambience.

"To us," Darnell said as they lifted flutes of sparkling grape juice.

"To us." Sammy gave him a loving smile.

"You do know what day this is."

"How could I forget? Your grandnephew and my younger cousins fixed us up on that blind date when I went to Atlanta. That was the start of something special."

"Indeed. When we started dating, I remember how concerned you were about how I'd adjust to life on a ranch after all those years in Paris. But that's only part of the reason we're here." Darnell's voice wavered a little.

Sammy reached out and took his hand. "I'm listening, honey."

"Sammy, we've had many years together. When Rene' died, it never occurred to me that I would find love again. I simply went on with life as a widower. Then, thanks to our meddling relatives, we

were brought together. I thank them for that. There are people out there who say gay men of a certain age can't find mates, and yet here we are. I can never replace John Lee, and you can never replace Rene', but together we've created new memories of us as a couple. They wouldn't have wanted us to be alone."

Sammy's eyes grew watery as Darnell continued, "I love you so much. I love the way I feel about myself when you're around. I love holding you in my arms. I love the touch of your lips on mine. I love how much you care for our horses and all the animals you've treated. I love the times we spend watching old movies after a long day of tending to the ranch. I love having you as a partner when we play Bid Whist with James and Lovell. I love the way your eyes crinkle up when you and Mister Magic have a moment. I love our circle of friends and family. Life didn't stop; it went on, and it became amazing.

"When we were young men, we never thought that one day we could legally marry. It seemed like an impossible dream. But now, the time is here. It's time to seize the moment."

Darnell lifted the cover dish that mysteriously appeared at their table to reveal a small velvet box. A tear trickled down Sammy's cheek when he opened it. Resting inside was a platinum ring, engraved with the infinity symbol and the words, 'My 2nd Chance.' His heart encouraged him as he looked deep into Sammy's eyes. "Samuel David Christopher, will you marry me?"

"In a heartbeat, Darnell Brian Smith," was Sammy's heartfelt reply. He extended his left hand for a euphoric Darnell to place the ring on his finger.

Their wedding was two years ago, during the window of opportunity when same-sex couples could marry in California. With the support of their ranch family and friends, they drove into San Bernardino in their classic 1965 Buick Wildcat to the county clerk's office, ready to apply for their marriage license. One phone call to Beckley brought the entire Christopher clan to California where they had a beautiful outdoor ceremony at the ranch on July 26,

2008. Beckley proudly stood up for his brother as best man while best friend James Wilson stood up for Darnell. By this time, Bernie, Sherman, and their sons had established their residence there, their new house having been completed on the property the previous year. Inspired by Sammy and Darnell's joy and happiness, James and Lovell Wilson were married two weeks later.

Proposition Eight, of course, made national news. At the time, the only saving grace about the whole affair was that their marriage, as well as the thousands of couples who tied the knot before it went into effect, remained valid. In the midst of the mess, one thing kept them hopeful: the conversation he had with Eli at their wedding. How it would play out was unknown, but he knew the power of his cousin's visions.

And it was playing out. Currently, five states and D.C. had marriage equality.

Even now, the matching wedding ring on his husband's hand and the familiar cadence of his slumber warmed him. Darnell had turned 90 earlier in the year, and aside from the usual "senior moments," his mind was still sharp, something neither of them took for granted. After saying a prayer of thanks for another day, he slipped into bed and spooned Darnell, gently running his hand over the shock of gray and white hair on the man he loved.

The next morning, after breakfast and chores, Sammy called Bernie over to the main ranch house. "What's up?" his nephew asked.

Sammy's eyes crinkled with a smile. "Bernie, you have been invaluable to me since you came into the practice. Your knowledge of horses has been the talk of the area, and you have more than proven yourself in gaining the trust of our clients. I'll still be around to look after our animals, but I want you to take over the practice, to run it as you see fit. I know I'm leaving it in good hands."

"Uncle Sammy, I…" For a man of 41 and standing at 6'8", Bernie could still be overwhelmed. He embraced his uncle in a gentle hug, doing his best to keep from turning on the waterworks full force. "Those horses will be so healthy they won't know what to do with themselves."

"That means everything to me, Bernie. And that's not all."

"There's more?"

"When your Uncle Darnell and I pass on, the ranch will go to you and Sherman."

"Oh, my God." Bernie's tears now flowed unchecked as he took Sammy in for another hug. "Trust and believe, we'll make you proud."

"I know you will." After allowing Bernie time to compose himself, Sammy let out a little chuckle. "You know, I see the way Sam is around our animals. You think he might be a chip off the old block?"

"Are you kidding me? Sam taking care of animals is like a kid in a candy store." Bernie reached down to scratch the head of his youngest son's tabby cat, Sanaa, while his beagle, Hershey, waited patiently. "When we lived in Chicago, he literally doted on these two. They're the most spoiled pets on the planet."

"It seems to me you've had your share of pets, too, like the one you took to your dad's office?" Sammy gave his nephew a naughty grin.

Bernie laughed at the memory of the havoc his pet gila monster created. "Yeah, Pepe was something else. It was years before Pops would even think about bringing me to the office again."

"So, he comes by it honestly."

Bernie smirked. "I know where you're going with this, Uncle Sammy. He just might become a vet. Animals are drawn to him."

"You know animals sense these things, Bernie. Sam has a good heart."

"Speaking of following in footsteps, I'm wondering when Mickey's going to join Sunrise."

"That depends on Lissa and Michael, particularly Michael. I noticed you didn't mention Little Allan."

Bernie scoffed. "I love my nephew, but you know the last time he sang, he ran the pets out of the room."

"Let's not take it that far, Bernie."

"Well, close enough. Anyway, Mickey has the talent a musician needs. We have to see if he can stand up under Michael's discipline."

Bernie stooped to give Hershey a doggie treat. "And Allan does possess a gift for songwriting, so Lissa and Michael may add some of his songs to their repertoire someday."

Sammy let out a mischievous chuckle. "I can imagine a certain person as the subject of several of Little Allan's songs."

"Tell me about it, Uncle. I can practically hear the wedding bells now. Ramsey Arrington has him securely on lockdown."

"Like you didn't waste time landing Sherman?"

Bernie chuckled. "Exactly."

"You might be right, especially with the way they looked at the Academy Awards show. The same with Mickey and Roslyn."

Bernie's grin became conspiratorial. "The way they look at each other with those heart eyes? No question about it. Somebody—or should I say, two somebodies—are going to put a ring on it, sooner than we think."

"What's this about putting a ring on it?" Darnell entered the family room with Sherman, greeting Sammy with a kiss.

"Hey, honey. We were just talking about Little Allan and Ramsey."

"Yeah. I don't think they're going to wait much longer to put out an engagement announcement," Bernie added, taking Sherman in his arms to share their own kiss.

"I agree. And soon, it'll be Jesse and Durrell tying the knot," Darnell teased.

"Please, he's only 17. Don't push it," Bernie cried dramatically at the mention of his oldest son and his boyfriend.

"Need I remind you how old we were when we jumped the broom?" Sherman joined in, his mischievous smile complimenting his dark brown complexion.

Lacking a rebuttal, Bernie could only laugh as the four men talked shop and shared family tidings.

Chapter 12

Fall 2010

The summers Allan worked at Christopher Electronics and Edwards Enterprises bore the fruit of permanent employment by the time fall rolled in. Impressed by the quality of his work, his cousin Eli Jr. brought him on board as a permanent hire upon his graduation. Allan knew going in that expectations would be high, just as they were with Aunt Vickie when she came into the company. She proved the skeptics and the chauvinists wrong when Grandpa Allan appointed her as CEO, and Allan too was committed to giving his professional best. Not that he was the only LGBT employee in the company—Aunt Vickie had been intentional in having LGBT representation in the thread of Christopher Electronics, from executives to management and on down.

As for Ramsey, his work and his work ethic was such that he was hired by Cousin Douglass at Edwards Enterprises where, under the mentoring of Cousin Darius, he was learning the ropes for a promising career in the field of high finance. The work was challenging, but Douglass and Darius also held to the motto that "happy people work harder," and the staff productivity proved it.

Thanksgiving gave Allan much to be thankful for. As he and Mickey enjoyed the festive meal with the Arringtons, he was grateful for his college degree, his position, his loving family, and most of all, finding the man who truly loved him as well as the woman who loved his twin. After three years, their relationships had only deepened and grown stronger. Ramsey's hand clasped his at the dining room table, followed by a warm smile when their eyes met. Mickey used his "Beckley eyes" to flirt with Roslyn, who was seated beside him. Rodney and Lanita, seated at the ends, pretended not to notice the young couples, even as they exchanged intuitive glances.

The next day, the couples were on a flight to Chicago, ready to spend the remainder of the Thanksgiving weekend with Lissa, Michael, and the rest of the Christophers. No sooner had they arrived then Ms. Bond had them seated at the dining room table with a multi-course banquet laid out before them waiting to be devoured. This year, Michael's mother Saralynne, brother Glenn, brother-in-law Jeffrey, and their 14-year-old son Curtis joined the family for dinner. Allan was glad the family already knew Ramsey and Roslyn; it was a sure bet that Uncle Jeffrey would have put them on blast otherwise.

Saturday, of course, was a time for shopping at the Oakbrook Terrace Mall. Understandably, it was packed, but the twins, their partners, and their cousins didn't care. For their parents, Water Tower Place and the shops around it was the ticket.

"You know, we'll need to get our trees soon," Allan noted while lugging his bag of presents.

"That shouldn't be a problem. We'll just make sure to do that when we get back." Mickey looked down at his own bag of gifts, thankful for the gift-wrapping service in the mall. "Dang. How are we going to get all this stuff on the plane? Especially since Roslyn shops 'til she drops?"

Allan thought for a moment. "Wait a minute. We're stressing out for nothing. All we have to do is ask Grandpa or Aunt Vickie."

"Yeah. Nothing like having access to a private jet when you need it. Anyway, I hope Ramsey and Roslyn are done soon since Grandpa and Grandma are expecting us."

"Look. Here they come." Allan recognized the truth in his twin's words when he saw the number of bags Roslyn was carrying. Ramsey's haul wasn't far behind. "Thank God we rented an SUV."

With three years of Minnesota winters under his belt, Allan considered himself an old pro at first, despite the skeptical looks he received from his older Edwards relatives. After all, he had actually lived through a winter when the temperature reached -22 and came out on the other side. Even so, he wasn't prepared for Saturday, December 11, 2010 and the 17 inches of snow it brought. All day long, the white stuff fell, slowly but surely burying the Twin Cities. On the occasions he peeked outside, Allan was grateful it was a weekend, and he could enjoy the time with family and with his bae. As Jermaine put it, "This is snuggling weather, and Marcellus and I are taking full advantage of it."

I just bet you will. Now that you're planning your own wedding, you'll take every opportunity. Allan chuckled softly as he curled up in a comforter in the living room, watching the *Soul Food* DVD from their collection. Ramsey had been in the bedroom on his laptop with the door closed, working on ideas for the creative team at work, time which Allan knew was sacrosanct. His mouth watered at the first Sunday dinner scene in the movie, wishing Ramsey could cook like that. *No, not going to happen anytime soon.* That level of cooking was something clearly in the territory of his grandmothers, his great-aunts, and Cousin Wayne. And Uncle Sammy and Uncle Darnell. Of course, Uncle Russell was a chef since Aunt Katie only knew her way around a microwave. After a while, the rumbling in his stomach from watching the family onscreen devouring that sinfully delicious food became too much. Reluctantly getting up, he headed to the kitchen to prepare a plate of the leftover roast beef dinner he had cooked for them.

He's been in there such a long time; it's high time he had something to eat, Allan thought, grabbing another plate to prepare Ramsey a helping. Placing the meal and a glass of grape juice on a tray, he walked down the hallway to the bedroom. Knocking on the door, he called out, "Bae, I have some food for you. You need to eat."

He could have sworn he heard shuffling around behind the door before he heard Ramsey answer, "You're right, boo. Come on in."

Balancing the tray, Allan managed to open the door, fully expecting to see books, notebooks, and papers scattered everywhere while Ramsey was bent over his laptop, burning the evening oil. Instead, his jaw dropped as he took in the surroundings. The bedroom was spotless, with scented candles strategically placed around the room. Softly playing in the background was an oldie-but-goodie, All 4 One's "I Swear." And Ramsey, his Ramsey, was dressed in a comfortable but sexy Timberwolves warm-up outfit…down on one knee, holding a small velvet box.

Allan was overwhelmed. He didn't know how he managed to set the tray on the floor, fighting back tears while Ramsey's eyes rested on him with all the love in his heart.

"Boo, I know your road wasn't always easy, what with dudes who wouldn't stand by you or dudes who only wanted something from you." Ramsey's voice was warm. "I only wish that I could have been there during those times. You are such an amazing man. You deserve forever, and I want so much to be the man by your side. If I have anything to say about it, no one will ever hurt you again. I want to share a home, a life, and kids with you. My heart is already yours. So is my love for you. That being said, boo, will you marry me?"

Wiping tears with his right hand and extending his left hand, Allan cried out, "Yes. *Yes!*"

After placing the beautiful engagement ring on his fiance's hand, Ramsey pulled Allan in for a heart-pounding, soul-stirring kiss as the lyrics from "I Swear" struck home in a powerful way. A winter storm may have been raging outside, but in their apartment, love was overflowing.

Dinner was heartily consumed in fortification for a love workout. Clothes slipped from their bodies with the ease of scented oil. Heated kisses, titillating touches, musical love ballads, and tongues savoring hot holes worked Ramsey and Allan into the joining they savored this night. Ramsey's long, deep thrusts, claiming Allan's big booty in a new way, sent Allan's head rocking to and fro on the pillows, coaxing unmistakable moans from his mouth.

"I love you. I love you. I love you. Fuck me. Keep fucking me. My ass belongs to you, bae. Take it."

"I love you too, boo."

"Say it again."

"I love you, boo. Man, it feels so good to be inside you. Your name is written all over my dick."

"Ooooh, I feel it. So fucking big, and it feels...yes!"

Allan's toes curled, a sign Ramsey knew warned of an imminent orgasm. His dick leaked copiously, throbbing and ready. "Bae...I'm gonna...gonna..."

He cried out in ecstasy as his orgasm swamped him. His dick turned into a cannon, drenching him with shot after shot of his nut while his anal walls clenched Ramsey's overheated dick. Mere seconds later, Ramsey's release filled him up, even as Ramsey's lips claimed his again, the sheen of their sweat joining them in yet another way.

The next morning, after a sultry, sensuous shower with his fiance, Allan left the bathroom and plopped down on the bed, barely covered by a towel, followed by a still amorous Ramsey. "You just can't keep your hands off my booty, can you?" Allan teased.

"You know you love it when I'm inside you," was Ramsey's sexy reply, lifting Allan's towel and caressing the aforementioned body parts. "And I can tell you want me up in there again."

Allan pushed his ass back against Ramsey's hand in confirmation. "Mmmmm," he sighed. "Just like I know how much your booty loves my dick. Like you said, it has my name written all over it. And your kisses..."

Ramsey let out a sexy chuckle. "See? We're made for each other."

At that moment, a familiar ringtone came from Allan's cell phone. "It's Mickey. Let me get this, and I promise you'll get some more later."

"You know I'll hold you to that." Ramsey gave him a disarming grin just before he playfully slapped his cakes.

Allan pressed the keypad to accept the call. "Hey, Mickey."

"She said yes! She said yes!" Mickey shouted.

"Hold on, hold on. Who said…" Allan's mouth broke out into a smile. "She did? *Congratulations!"*

"Thanks, man. Asking Roslyn to marry me was the smartest thing I've ever done."

"I hear you, Mickey, and you deserve it. And she's not the only one who said yes."

"Are you saying…"

"Ramsey put a ring on it last night."

"Get outta here!!!"

"Yes, he did. Looks like great minds think alike."

"What? What?" Ramsey broke in.

Momentarily, Allan turned from the phone to his fiancé. "Mickey proposed to Roslyn. She said yes."

"What?!" he exclaimed, running to his phone.

"What's going on over there?" Mickey asked.

"That was Ramsey. I'm sure he's on the phone with Roslyn right now getting all the juicy details."

"I'm sure. Anyway, as soon as we can dig our way out, we need to get together and celebrate."

"Why don't you come over here? You know the parking's better. How about tomorrow? It's not like anything's gonna be open with this much snow."

"I'll run it by Roslyn and call you back to confirm."

Allan peeked down the hallway where an animated Ramsey conversed on his cell phone with his twin. "That sounds like a plan."

Chapter 13

2011

With the euphoria of marriage proposals in the air after a good meal, the couples met with smiles of an unspoken, shared thought. Roslyn was the first to break the ice. "Are you guys thinking what I'm thinking?"

"I bet we are," Allan replied with a grin that only grew bigger. "A double wedding."

"There you go."

Mickey and Ramsey nodded in hearty agreement. "Now that that's settled, we have to decide on the where," Ramsey said.

Roslyn gave her twin a mock incredulous look. "Where else, my dear brother? In New York—at the Plaza Hotel."

"Great minds think alike," Allan beamed. "Like you said, Mickey, marrying Roslyn is going to be the smartest thing you've ever done."

Mickey cast adoring eyes at his fiancée and went in for a loving kiss. "Tell me about it."

Ramsey followed suit with an arm around Allan's waist and squeezing him affectionately. "It's a good thing New York is putting marriage equality into law. With all those PSAs on TV, it's on its way. I say we get married in July."

"Any particular reason, bae?" Allan purred.

Ramsey peered over at his sister and they shared a wink. "Well-l-l-l…July is a special month, after all."

Mickey immediately picked up the obvious hint as he held Roslyn in his arms. "Then it's done. For the two special people in our lives, that's when we'll tie the knot. In the meantime, we have some breaking news to share."

The couples wasted no time navigating the snow-covered streets and highways to visit Ramsey and Roslyn's parents in Arden Hills. When Allan and Roslyn flashed their engagement rings, one could have sworn Rodney and Lanita won the Minnesota State Lottery. "As Grandpa would say, 'You done good,'" was Rodney's hearty endorsement as he embraced the couples while Lanita alternated between crying and jumping up and down with joy, followed by snow showers of hugs and kisses.

"Have you told your parents yet?" Lanita managed to ask after she was able to compose herself—somewhat.

"No, you're the first ones to know," was Allan's reply.

"Well, what are you waiting for?" Lanita raced to the desktop computer. "Let's tell them now!"

Normally, Lissa never put down a Sylvia Berry Lewis novel she was engrossed in, and this was a good one: *The Case of the Good-for-nothing Gigolo.* However, her intuition and curiosity got the best of her when she looked up and noticed the indicator on the desktop monitor. Skype call from the Arringtons. "Lanita. What's going on?" she asked.

"Hey, Lissa. Is Michael there?"

"He's in the studio."

"Go get him."

"What?"

"Just go get him," Lanita urged. "Trust me, you *want* to hear this news!"

Dragging Michael out of an instrumental rehearsal with the guys was no easy feat, but she did it. Literally taking him by the hand to the den, they sat in front of their computer monitor. "All right. We're here. Now what is this all about?"

"Yeah," Michael insisted. "What is so important?"

"Just this." Lanita gave them the smile of someone holding a royal flush in a poker game. "Allan, Roslyn, show them."

Michael's jaw dropped, and Lissa's hands went to her face. "Oh, my God. Yes. *Yes!!"* she cried out, the sparkle of the engagement rings telling all.

"I told you you'd want to hear this news," Lanita gloated.

"OK, you got us," Michael conceded with a grin. "Now, do you have a date and a venue?"

"We want to get married in July. In New York. At the Plaza," Allan answered. "Oh, one more thing…"

"What's that?"

"We've decided on a double wedding." Roslyn's smile refused to come off.

Lissa's heart melted with the news as she heard Lanita gushing with happiness over the wedding plans. She easily empathized with her; it was enough to make any mother positively giddy. How many women had dreamed of a wedding there, much less an LGBT couple? This was a mountain that must be moved, and whatever it took for their children to have the wedding of their dreams, they would do it. From the expression that she and Lanita shared momentarily, not only were they on the same page, but the same paragraph.

Allan truly appreciated the motto, "Family is everything" when it came to the planning phase. No doubt, wedding planners across the U.S. would have killed for the prestige of having this wedding in their portfolios. However, the couples didn't have to look any further than Allan and Mickey's cousin, Willona Loomis Hendricks. Her services were sought after nationwide, and her schedule stayed booked, yet she humbly and gladly accepted the job. Better still, while visiting another cousin, Jerome Franklin-Edwards his husband Ariel one day, a strange look clouded over Jerome's eyes. When he came to, he told them, "July 24. That's when you're getting married."

"But marriage equality there hasn't – " Ramsey started.

"That won't be a problem. The governor will sign the law in June. It'll go into effect July 24."

Ramsey was shocked. "How do you know this?"

Ariel, who had been giving their younger daughter Linda a bottle, explained, "Jerome inherited the gift from his Grandpa Eli, too, having visions of things before they happen. They're random, and they occur once in a while. But when they do, they *always* come to pass."

"In other words, our wedding date is locked down. Wait'll we tell Mickey and Roslyn."

Seven months was short in wedding time. There was so much planning to do, but with Willona sharing their vision and in charge of the details, and their mothers an integral part of the process, it was more fun and less challenging. They had already agreed that Allan and Mickey's cousin, Rev. Darrell Edwards, would be the officiant, a position which was wholeheartedly accepted.

"Now, you have the date and your officiant. Before we discuss the theme, let's discuss the venue," Willona stated during their first consultation.

The couples exchanged uncertain glances. "What is it?" Willona asked.

"The thing is, we have our hearts set on the Plaza Hotel," Roslyn said.

"We've been concerned about getting it. Reservations for weddings there take such a long time," Allan added.

Willona merely replied, "Let me make a phone call. Would you step out for a moment?" Ten minutes later, she called them back into her office. "You're booked."

Their wedding plans also included periodic trips to New York, one of the most important ones being a trip to Kleinfeld's to shop for Roslyn's wedding gown. Lanita, Lissa, Grandma Maureen, Allan, and Roslyn's BFF's had accompanied her. After trying on a couple of dresses, Roslyn stepped out in a showstopping princess gown by Pnina Tornai. It was an excellent blend of sexy, elegant, and princess in design, with the right amount of bling on the sweetheart bodice.

"Roslyn, that's your dress," Allan beamed. "When Mickey sees you, it'll knock his socks off."

"Baby, you are absolutely beautiful," Lanita gushed, her eyes misty.

After the veil was placed on her head, Roslyn turned to her reflection in the mirror. Her breath caught in her throat for a moment, and her eyes were misty. "I feel so beautiful. I feel sexy, I feel like a princess. It all feels real now. I feel…like a bride. I *love* this dress."

"And it shows," Lissa added.

Lanita, her heart washing over with the emotions all mothers experience when their daughters are about to be wed, had tears in her eyes when she embraced her daughter. "Your father is going to be so proud when he walks you down the aisle. And Mickey…well, you will blow him away." Lanita looked back at Lissa, who had teared up as well. "Now, I'm sure Kleinfeld's has a reception dress that's right for you. Are you ready?"

"Mom, I'm more than ready," Roslyn beamed.

With his future sister-in-law's dresses chosen, Allan met with one of the designers in the store for a showstopper of his own. When the sketch was completed, Lissa viewed it and gave her son a big hug. "Allan, I love it. It's you. It's totally you."

She passed the sketch to her mother, who nodded in assent. "Come here, Little Allan," she said, wrapping him up in a grandma hug. "When you walk down that aisle with your dad, you will make us proud."

"And we promise not to tell Ramsey a thing. When my son sees you, he won't help but fall more in love with you." Lanita joined the women, embracing Allan in a group hug.

Given the special bond he shared with Grandma Maureen since his day at Lake Superior, Allan was overwhelmed. "Thank you, Grandma, Mom, Mama Lanita."

Like millions of people around the world, Allan, Ramsey, Mickey, and Roslyn were glued to a flat-screen television set to witness the wedding of Prince William and Kate Middleton on April 29, 2011. They, however, had an inside track. The twins' cousin Veronica and her husband, Lord Nigel Moriarty, were guests to the event.

"Look at Kate. She is every inch a queen. And William won't be able to keep his eyes off her," Roslyn gushed.

Mickey wrapped his arm around his fiancée'. "So are you, baby. So are you."

Ramsey shifted to a more comfortable position in Allan's arms. "And look at it this way. In three months, we'll have our own version of a royal wedding."

"Speaking of which, where are we at so far as guests?" Allan asked.

Roslyn thought for a moment. "Well, excluding our wedding party, between family, friends, family friends, industry names, and celebrities, we're at 700 people."

Mickey let out a low whistle. "And they all did the RSVP?"

Roslyn nodded, glancing back at the television for a moment. "Ms. Hendricks said the replies came in faster than a sold-out concert for Sunrise."

"I'm glad we have her," Allan mused. "Planning our wedding would have been a lot more stressful without her."

"Yeah. If we're going through this, imagine what it was like for them." Ramsey took in the sheer volume of guests inside Westminster as Michael Middleton processed down the aisle with his daughter.

"Of course, we have an advantage. We won't have just one queen at our wedding. Our mothers will truly be queens that day. Plus, we have plenty of LGBT queens on the guest list," Mickey declared with a grin.

"Looking fierce and fabulous," Ramsey emphasized to the cheers of the couples before they settled in to continue viewing the royal wedding.

Although the dresses for the female attendants and the tuxes for the male attendants in the wedding party went smoothly, it was the catering that ran into roadblocks. From the two couples came four different and strong opinions on the menu for the sit-down dinner. In addition, with the two wedding cakes, neither couple could agree on the flavor for each. As a result, Allan, Ramsey, Mickey, and Roslyn left the tasting sessions full, on sugar overload, and barely speaking to each other.

Phone calls to parents and other relatives left the couples with the same answer, epitomized by Rodney Arrington: "We love you, and we understand your frustration, but this is your wedding. You should know by now that being in a relationship is constant negotiation. Marriage only continues the process. It's up to you to come together with something you all can live with."

Left to their own devices, they managed to turn to one another and say, "I'm sorry." Over the next few days, they finally agreed upon a menu, followed by the cakes.

For Lissa and her siblings, returning to New York also included reconnecting with their Uncle Mitch, his wife Delores, and their Moore cousins. Mother had shared the family stories about her twin brother when she became an adult, and how for so long, he was considered the ne'er-do-well of the family. Lissa had only known him as the upstanding man he was today, but she was shocked that it had taken his first wife's death to do it. Not only that, he had played a role in nearly causing Mother to divorce Father while they lived in Brooklyn 60 years ago.

Regarding her uncle now, an 82-year-old man and a church trustee, Lissa realized that, like Father, he too had had to deal with unforgiveness, especially with himself. Maybe he felt he couldn't live up to the standards her grandparents set as educators who were well respected in the community, turning instead to alcohol, gambling, womanizing, and cheating. "Allison, when your Aunt Dinah died in that car accident, he was a hot mess. They were going to take Diane and Marlena away from him," Mother shared with her after their visit. "No one could get through to him, but somehow your father did. He never told me what he said, but your Uncle Mitch was a different man after that. And then he met your Aunt Delores, which was another major step on the road to becoming the man he was meant to be. He's made a good life for himself and his family, and I couldn't be prouder of him."

"God definitely turned his life around, Mother," Lissa concluded.

"Amen."

Camaraderie flowed at the rehearsal dinner, and Allan was caught up in it. During the middle of it all, he heard his Grandpa Allan say, "To our soon-to-be-newlyweds, we wish you all the happiness in the world. And to that end, your mothers have something they want to share with you."

At that moment he heard an instrumental soundtrack play, while Lissa and Lanita began a duet. The entire room quieted as they sang Regina Belle's rendition of "If I Could." His eyes soon grew misty, and then the tears flowed. Ramsey was no better, nor Mickey and Roslyn. It didn't stop there. Every parent in the room had teared up, so powerful were the emotions stirred as their mothers sang from their hearts. When they finished the song, no power on earth could have stopped their children from running to them as those in attendance heartily applauded and cheered.

Chapter 14

July 2011

Allan really didn't understand the tradition of not seeing Ramsey the night before the wedding, having lived together for the past three years. To humor his parents and his soon-to-be in-laws, he went along with it, since Roslyn already required it of Mickey. His steps were light with anticipation as he walked up Fifth Avenue to the Plaza Hotel to meet with Cousin Willona for a few last-minute details. In addition, he and Ramsey would make sure they were at the county building early enough tomorrow to get a good place in line, since the wedding was scheduled for seven p.m. He never knew how Madear had arranged for them to receive a judicial waiver of the 24-hour waiting period once they signed their marriage license. All he knew was that with her, things had a way of happening. For that, he was eternally grateful.

Just before he entered the hotel, someone behind him called out, "Allan!" Although he hadn't heard that voice in five years, he instinctively knew it wasn't a figment of his imagination. He turned around in time to face a man from out of his past.

"Thomas," he said. "How are you?"

Still wrapping his mind around Thomas Hamilton approaching him, Allan studied his face. It bore the world-weariness of one who'd been through an ordeal, and yet it held a certain peace. "It's good to see you, Allan. As for me, things are better now."

"What do you mean by better?"

"Can we talk?"

Allan hesitated. "I have to meet with my wedding planner in a bit."

"I know. Your wedding has been blogged all over the entertainment industry, and I'm truly happy for you and your fiancé. I promise, this will only take a few minutes."

"Well…all right. Let's step inside."

After finding a semi-private spot in the lobby, Allan and Thomas took seats. Curiosity ate at Allan over this unexpected meeting with his ex, the man who swore up and down that he would never leave the islands. Sitting quietly, he waited for Thomas to speak.

"First of all, I want to ask your forgiveness for the way I hurt you, the way I allowed my fear to hurt you and any possibility of us having a relationship back then," Thomas said humbly. "I was so terrified of accepting who I am and coming out, and I tried to control you. I realize the reasons I gave you were all just excuses—a person who loves another doesn't try to hide him or deny him. You were already having problems on the island because of how you were treated, and I only added to them by not standing up for you. Anyway, after you left, things went downhill for me. I drank and drank. My bills fell further and further behind. Soon my drinking affected my job, to the point where I was relieved of duty.

"I didn't care. I hated myself. I would pick up men for a one-off and go on to the next, never giving out any information because I was afraid that they would out me. And I'd drink some more." Despite his astonishment, Allan nodded in understanding while Thomas continued his story. "One night, a man I picked up took me to a party. I was already drunk by then, so I didn't really think about it. The party turned out to be a sex party. All the men there were turned on by the idea of fucking a cop—even an ex-cop. And even the men who hated cops. Every guy there fucked me, once, twice, maybe three times, I don't know; at the time I was too drunk to even care. When I did come to, I was somewhere outside in the bushes, naked, hung over, practically covered in dried semen from head to toe. At that moment, I knew I had hit bottom, and I needed help.

"It wasn't easy to admit I'm an alcoholic, but I got the help I needed. You know, when I was a police officer, I always had to be in charge, in authority, and in total control. The only place I could surrender that control was in the bedroom. Well, I've learned that that's not true. I can also surrender control to my Higher Power." Thomas took a moment for a cleansing breath. "I've been sober for three years now, and I go to meetings every week, sometimes every day if I need to. That gave me the courage to do the very thing I'd been afraid to do. I came out."

For a moment, Allan wondered if he'd been transported to some parallel universe, but he remained calm and attentive. "You did? How did it go?"

"Better than I thought. The people I came out to didn't judge me or any of that. You were right about feeling better about myself; I can see that now. I moved to New York…"

"You what?"

"Yes, Allan. I live here in New York. I'm working in security detail now. I have a great support group, and nine months ago…I met someone."

Allan's mind buzzed with all the revelations. "Don't leave me hanging now, Thomas. Tell me about him."

"Well, his name is Jamarius. He's 31, and he's a stockbroker. He looks something like that actor Taye Diggs, only he's taller. When we realized things were getting serious, I told him I was a recovering alcoholic. He joined the family group. Like everything else, we're taking our relationship one day at a time, but there is definitely hope for a future with him."

"Have you met his family?"

"Yes. I was pretty nervous before I met them, but once I did, I really felt welcomed. I may not have that kind of support back on the islands, but I have it here."

"All I can say is, I'm happy things turned out well for you, Thomas. You deserve happiness," Allan said sincerely as he gave Thomas a hug.

With all his errands completed, Allan joined Mickey for their joint bachelor party that evening, hosted by their relatives, some college classmates, plus Dylan and Hari. Given the scheduling of Allan's early wake-up call, it was agreed that the party would end at midnight. Early on in the festivities, Allan took the opportunity to pull Mickey aside, eager to share.

"Mickey, you won't believe who I saw today outside the Plaza."

"All right, I'm game. Who?"

"Thomas Hamilton."

Mickey gave his brother an incredulous look. "Are you kidding me?"

"I wish I were, but it was Thomas."

"What's he doing here? Did that chump give you any trouble?"

"Actually, he lives here now. He asked my forgiveness for the way he treated me."

Mickey was skeptical. "Sounds like there's more to this story."

"Yes. He's a recovering alcoholic." When Allan finished telling Mickey the rest of Thomas' story, Mickey's eyebrows rose as he repeated, "Are you kidding me?"

"No. He's been through a lot, but he's finally living his truth."

"Does that like, mean he wants to get back in your life in some way?"

"I'd say it was more like closure, making amends. He has a boyfriend and he's happy, I have Ramsey and I'm happy, and we've each moved on with our lives."

"Cool. Hey, let's get back to the party before they put out an APB on us."

At five a.m. on Sunday, July 24, 2011, Allan and Ramsey arrived at the New York city clerk's office, figuring that would guarantee them a place at the front of the line. Apparently, others had the same idea. There was already a line of couples there, but not to the point of going down the street and reaching around the block. Witnessing couples from all ethnicities anxious to tie the knot after being together for years, even decades, they could well understand it. Celebration and anticipation filled the air as the waiting couples shared their stories. Allan had heard similar stories from Uncle Sammy and Uncle Darnell, now happily and legally married for three years, and he soaked them up with the capacity of new sponges.

The festive air increased once the doors opened. People cheered as one by one, couples who never dreamed this day would come entered and returned with marriage licenses in hand. The most touching moment was with the first couple, a white lesbian couple who had been together for more than 50 years and were married on the spot.

Sooner than anticipated, it was their turn. Encouraged by the couples behind them, Allan's internal butterflies kicked in as Ramsey took his hand and they approached the friendly Bette Midler lookalike behind the service desk, ready to apply.

"This just got real, bae." Allan's "Beckley eyes" glowed with warmth. "And I can hardly wait 'til this evening."

"That makes two of us, boo." Ramsey's hand intertwined with Allan's.

Cousin Willona had outdone herself with her skills as a wedding planner. With 700 guests and a high-profile wedding, she had, in Allan's mind, taken the ball and run with it. The results were awesome if the peek he took inside the ballrooms was any indication. Contemporary yet royal, the theme was skillfully interwoven throughout, all the way down to the place settings and the intricately designed "A & R/M & R" on the wedding favors. A smirk crossed his face as he pictured Cousin Brian—who would have had a coronary if he had been left off the guest list—fiercely guarding his share of mementos until he could take them home.

Cousin Willona was also a stickler for time. Anyone who wasn't seated at seven p.m. didn't get in, and they would be subject to removal from the premises by security if the tardy guest made a scene. Needless to say, everyone was prompt and in their seats when Rev. Edwards took his place at the altar, the signal for the music to begin the processional.

Grandpa Allan was totally in his glory with Grandma Maureen by his side. Grandma Saralynne was ecstatic. Small wonder. A week before the wedding, Lissa sat the twins down during a visit to Uncle Mitch and Aunt Delores. "When I was engaged to your father, your grandfather wanted a high-profile wedding for us, with celebrities, media coverage, the works. However, we wanted a wedding at home, and that was right for us. Well, Father finally got his wish through the two of you. You have no idea how over-the-moon he's feeling right now, and how proud he is of you."

Allan had seen the wedding photos of his cousins and his uncles, and how sharp they were in their tuxes. He could appreciate the look, but he had wanted something a little more dramatic for himself, something special for his future husband to see only when he walked down the aisle. Hence, he chose a form-fitting white tux with an African-print kufi to crown his freshly done waist-length dreadlocks plus a matching cummerbund. Topping it off, courtesy of his day at Kleinfeld's, was a flowing white mantle with a train, complete with serious bling. Processing down the aisle with his proud father, the comments of the guests plus the look on Ramsey's face was confirmation that it had all been worth it. He had taken his man's breath away.

Ramsey possessed the air of a Rastafarian prince waiting for his prince. During the time they had been together, he let his dark brown hair grow out to dreadlocks that rested just below his shoulders. Dressed in a classic white tux, he was drop-dead sexy. But it was the expression of awe and love in his eyes that drew Allan to him with each step, moments that would be engraved in his mind forever.

Mickey, sporting a black tux with red highlights, gave his twin a look when he reached the altar as if to say, "Yeah, you showed up and showed out." However, his jaw dropped when Roslyn appeared on the arm of her beaming father and began her procession down the aisle. She looked like a goddess. If he wasn't already besotted with her, this would have sealed the deal. He knew she had gone to Kleinfeld's, accompanied by his mother, his mother-in-law, his grandmother, her best friends, and Allan to buy her dress, and none of them would give him any information. From the way she glowed, she had given it an emphatic yes. Wow! Without a doubt, in a wedding filled with family, celebrities, and VIPs, Roslyn and Allan were the undisputed center of attention.

Allan may have had the talent for songwriting and other areas, but he had learned long ago that singing wasn't one of them. Mickey had, at one point, told him, "I hate to say this, but you sing like a cat whose tail had been stepped on." Fortunately, Cousin Wayne was more than happy to sing the love song Allan had written just for Ramsey during the ceremony, as well as the one he wrote especially for Roslyn from Mickey. During the songs, his father caught his eye and winked.

"By the power vested in me by God and the state of New York, I hereby pronounce you married. Allan, Ramsey, Michael, Roslyn, you may kiss your spouses."

Ramsey held Allan in his arms and kissed him tenderly, lovingly, the kind of kiss that was public yet intimate at the same time. They heard the applause—and sniffles—around them. This kiss was different from all the kisses they had shared before now. The fact that Ramsey was his husband took it to a new level. They had claimed each other, now and forever.

Darrell smiled beatifically as he announced, "I proudly present to you for the first time, Roslyn and Michael Davis, Jr., and Allan and Ramsey Arrington-Davis." Amidst the applause and cheers for the newlywed couples, he placed the ceremonial broom on the aisle. The couples jumped it with ease, generating more cheers.

Allan was on a high as he and Ramsey followed their siblings up the aisle hand in hand, looking out on the abundance of family and well-wishers, exchanging loving glances at his new husband. The smile on his face simply refused to come off. No longer was he that 17-year-old who doubted he'd ever find love. This was a new day, the first day of the rest of his life, with Ramsey by his side. The fact that Mickey had also found his soulmate in Roslyn and was sharing this day only made everything better.

While the guests engaged in more socializing and schmoozing, the wedding party was whisked off to another area of the hotel for the formal wedding pictures and the signing of the marriage certificates, after which Roslyn excused herself to change into her stunning reception dress. Though he was famous for his work in fashion photography, Uncle Travis' skills gave the edge to photographs the couples would treasure.

The ballroom décor for the reception continued the unique wedding theme. The attention to detail was amazing, something the newlyweds made sure to thank Cousin Willona for profusely before they made their entrance.

Many of their older relatives teared up when the newlywed couples danced their first dance, for they chose the Flamingos' version of "I Only Have Eyes For You." For the dances with their parents, they had requested Natalie Cole's "Inseparable." At different times during the dance, Michael and Rodney danced with their sons, to which they heard "Awwww."

"You're married now, Allan Arrington-Davis," Michael said proudly. "May you two have every happiness. You deserve it."

Allan beamed at hearing his new surname. "Thanks, Dad. Uncle Sammy said I needed a ride-or-die guy, and I found him in Ramsey."

Michael's eyes scanned the ballroom until he spotted the table where Uncle Sammy and Uncle Darnell were seated. With full-wattage grins, they raised their flutes to them in support, as did Bernie and Sherman.

The reception was still going strong in full party mode when the couples quietly slipped away after dancing to their theme song: Beyonce' and Jay-Z's "Crazy In Love." Allan held Ramsey in his arms, kissing him passionately in the middle of their honeymoon suite, grinding his erection against his spouse's. After four years, they knew each other's bodies quite intimately. This night, however, that simple "I do" took their intimacy to a new level. Breaking the kiss, they undressed each other quickly but not frantically, pupils dilating with desire at the sight of each other.

His sandy-brown dreadlocks fanned out on the king-sized bed, legs held against his chest and love tunnel lubed and ready, Allan moaned in sheer bliss as Ramsey entered him. Being filled by the man he loved only made his dick harder as Ramsey made sweet, sweet love to him. "Don't stop. Please don't stop," Allan cried softly as his husband rocked his hips in that way of his which was guaranteed to hit his P-spot. Ramsey's intimate knowledge served him well, for he knew many ways to bring Allan to the edge and then pull him back. Allan thought he would go out of his mind with pleasure as Ramsey, now his for life, thrust deeper and hotter into him. Just before Allan's dick became slick with fluid and imminent release, Ramsey pulled out of him, dick wet and throbbing, his eyes glazed with lust and love.

"Your turn," he said in a voice husky with passion and need. Allan smiled with anticipation as Ramsey got on his hands and knees and quickly lubed his hole, twerking his luscious booty the way Allan loved to see it. In one easy, long thrust, Allan took him from behind, relaxing and yet stimulating Ramsey to the point where he could pull all the way out and enter him again—and again—and again.

It was only a matter of minutes before Ramsey cried out, "I love you, boo. Boo, I'm gonna…gonna…" Allan felt his dick squeezed as jets of cum shot from Ramsey's shaft, coating the sheets beneath him. That was all it took for Allan to let loose with his own powerful release, filling his new husband with his seed.

Caught up in the blissful haze of afterglow, Ramsey held Allan tenderly, giving him that well-loved smile of his. "You know, boo, it's even better legal."

"You don't say?" Allan laughed softly, knowing the truth in those words.

"And this…is only the beginning of our wedding night."

Allan felt his freshly fucked hole twitch at the thought of another round of lovemaking, while his penis showed renewed signs of stirring. "Bring it on, bae. Bring it on. But first…"

"Yes?"

"I do believe I hear a big tub filled with bubble bath and body oil calling us."

“I like the way you think,” was Ramsey’s sexy reply as the two headed for the bathroom.

After a leisurely soak in the sumptuous bathtub, accentuated by the scented almond candles and soothing bath oil, the newlyweds dried each other off with fluffy bath towels, enjoying a brief midnight snack before Ramsey took Allan again, savoring the feel of Allan’s internal walls around his tool of passion. They could go from fucking like rabbits to making sweet love, and this time his sweet lovemaking had Allan uttering the deep, sensual moans Ramsey loved to hear, the kind that told him Allan was his and only his. At least half the time, he could make Allan come just by fucking him. As he slowly turned up the heat, his dick massaging that special spot, Ramsey knew this would be one of those times. Sure enough, after increasing the tempo and hitting his P-spot in the right way, Allan flew apart untouched, and Ramsey was right there with him.

The following afternoon, the newlyweds arrived by limo at Kennedy International Airport, eager for their flights to transport them to their honeymoon destinations. For Mickey and Roslyn, it was off to the U.K.; for Allan and Ramsey, the U.S. Virgin Islands. Though they spent much of their time in their resort on St. Croix, the newlyweds would occasionally hop over to Charlotte Amalie on St. Thomas to take in the attractions and do their share of shopping. Still, the idyllic and relative seclusion of the resort enthralled them as nature lovers. It even gave them the opportunity to fulfill a fantasy of Ramsey’s.

“So, bae. What’s this fantasy you have?” Allan asked as they enjoyed the view from their suite.

“You know I was born and raised in Minnesota.”

“And?”

“And I’ve always loved nature, boo. I want to know what it’s like to make love on a tropical beach with you.”

Allan’s sultry, saucy reply was, “Convince me.”

Ramsey’s voice dropped to Barry White sensual level. “And how can I do that?”

“When we find a spot, I want you to take your clothes off, twerk your booty cheeks like you want it, and then spread them.” Allan could already feel his dick swelling.

“Is that all it takes, boo?” Ramsey backed his ass up against him. “Well, that’s one hot no-brainer.”

“Yes.” Allan shuddered with desire from the contact. “But you’re not the only one who gets to have all the fun, bae.”

Ramsey ground his bootylicious butt harder against Allan’s dick, which had turned to steel. “Oh, really?”

“Really. After I tell you how much I love you…while I come deep inside you…and fuck your love juice out of you…you get to lick my hole, so it’ll be all hot…and wet…and ready… for your big fuckin’ dick.” Between the kisses he planted on his neck, Allan reached around and leisurely stroked Ramsey’s throbbing shaft, which was now tenting his shorts. “After you recover, of course.” Allan stepped away from Ramsey and headed out the door, his dick a flagpole straining at his own shorts. Ramsey followed him with eyes overwhelming with lust.

Needless to say, the resulting experience was one the couple would place in their vault of treasured memories.

Chapter 15

March 2012

After their wonderful honeymoon, Allan and Ramsey settled into work and married life. Back at Christopher Electronics, Allan received his share of support and congratulations on his engagement and wedding rings while handling his duties in the accounting department and pondering his future. His grandfather, of course, was all for having him work his way up the ranks. Aunt Vickie had complimented him on his work ethic, with a hearty endorsement from his cousin, Eli Edwards, Jr.

Though working his way up in the company to a front office had its appeal, Allan's sights were set on becoming part of the philanthropic branch. The Lorraine Beckley Christopher Scholarship Fund started it all back in 1974, and he could already envision grants and donations to support facilities and programs for homeless LGBT youth with the dream of a day when such shelters were no longer needed. He planned to have a meeting with Aunt Vickie about it in the near future.

Fully settling in, however, had the added factor of their current status in the media spotlight. The twins, along with their parents and patriarch Allan Beckley Christopher, had already been approached to do public service announcements in support of marriage equality as well as appear on talk shows and news interviews. Wisely, they deferred to Okeidi's judgment, choosing journalists and hosts who had been consistently supportive over the years. On the talk shows the couples appeared on, the hosts heartily played up the twins-marrying-twins angle and their double wedding. By choosing to do the PSAs as a family and as part of Sunrise, their families sent a strong message, as evidenced by the letters and emails of support they received over the next several months.

As much as he enjoyed his current position, Allan still loved writing songs, and he was pleased that his father had accepted some of his songs for his mother to sing with Sunrise. "These songs have it all, son," Michael told him, smiling. "They have heart, thought, and a message. Songs like these endure the test of time."

"Got that right." Ronnell Austin-Hayes and Michael drew Allan in for a group hug. "You know, if you ever decide to do it, you could make a career out of songwriting. And you will receive royalties for these songs."

"Thanks," Allan replied. "That's good to know. So, Dad, when will Mickey come on board with Sunrise?"

"All in good time, son," Michael replied cryptically. "All in good time."

Allan left the office after a mentally challenging day of number-crunching and administrative duties, wanting nothing more than to relax and connect with his husband. Rather than navigate the usual rush-hour traffic on Hiawatha Avenue, he chose the quieter scenic route along West River Parkway. He took advantage of the slower speed limit to check out the houses along the parkway, contemplating the plans they had started for actively buying their own home. He really needed to step up his game; Roslyn was already after Mickey in the house-hunting department, from the conversations they had been having when the couples got together.

He was thankful to find an available parking space near their apartment building on East 46th Street and 46th Avenue South. After closing the car door, he took a quick stretch, savoring the 70-plus temperatures that had graced March and brought everyone out of hibernation. He didn't see Ramsey's Honda Pilot during his walk to the building, but he knew it wouldn't be long before his husband arrived home so they could catch up on their respective days. Hopefully, that would be followed by their favorite form of tension relief. Already he could visualize Ramsey's expert hands roaming over his body while his hole winked with the need to be filled and plowed by his hot, sexy husband to passionate satisfaction. Fortunately for him, no one was in the immediate vicinity to see his dick swell at the amorous thought.

Allowing the relaxing aura of their apartment to envelop him, Allan toed off his shoes inside the door, heading to the bedroom where he changed into comfortable black sweatpants and a U of M jersey. He normally loved hearing KMOJ on the radio, but not at six o'clock, so he opted for some New Age instrumental music. Ramsey had made a huge lasagna dinner the night before, which he placed in the oven to warm up. *He's certainly gotten better about cooking since we were married.* A garden salad was next on the menu, which helped him leave his workday at work and keep him in the present. He finished making the salad and placed it in the refrigerator when he heard a distinctive ringtone on his phone.

"Hey Mickey, what's up."

"Allan, are you sitting down?"

"No."

"Well, sit yourself down, 'cause you aren't going to believe this."

Allan found a spot on the sofa. "All right. I'm sitting. Spill."

"Well, he finally did it."

"Who did what?"

"Dad. I'll be playing with Sunrise for their next concert in May."

"Shut *up!!*" Allan exclaimed. "Where? Where?"

"Here, and then Milwaukee, Chi-town, and Indy."

"I am so thrilled for you. I know how long you've been waiting for Dad to give you the green light. And now it's happening. What did Roslyn say?"

"She said, 'You tell me when. I'll take care of the rest.' I'm taking her out to dinner tonight to celebrate. So you're going to be there?"

"Please. Tell me you did not just ask me that," Allan scoffed.

"Oh…there's more." Mickey's tone was mysterious.

"More? What do you mean, more?"

"The repertoire's going to include some of the songs you wrote."

Allan was stunned. "Wow."

"That means you have to be there. Hey, my wife's waiting for me to wine and dine her. Gotta go…"

"Wait! What about Grandma Maureen? If you don't tell her, you'll never hear the end of it."

"Mom already told her. Of course, she and Grandpa Allan and Grandma Saralynne get VIP treatment. Can't keep Roslyn waiting. Gotta go!"

Even with the insider knowledge that accompanies being a child of entertainment royalty, Mickey was nervous on opening night at Orchestra Hall. Everything he so painstakingly rehearsed nearly flew right out the window as he stood backstage, the curtain ready to go up in fifteen minutes. The lighting and sound checks had since been completed, but as he sat there in his Afro-Caribbean attire in the green room, he found himself wondering, *What in the world am I doing here?*

"Mickey…."

He snapped out of his trance. "Oh. Dad."

"It's OK to be a little nervous on gigs like this. It gives you just enough of an edge to do your best. That's how I felt; so did your mother and the guys. The thing is not to let it get into your head."

"But what if I make a mistake?"

"So you make a mistake. But you keep on going. Nine times out of ten, your audience won't even realize you have unless you call attention to it. God only knows it's happened to me enough times." Michael put his hands on his son's shoulders, detecting the tension in his muscles. "I know you think I'm a stickler for perfection, and to a certain extent I am. But your mom taught me something to do when my nerves go over the top. Before she goes onstage, she takes some time to breathe and center herself. She's probably doing that now. So, let's practice this. And while we are, remember the people who love you and have prayers of good success for you."

"Thanks, Dad." Mickey was still nervous but in a good way as he began the breathing exercises.

The applause of the sold-out crowd at Orchestra Hall became an adrenaline rush when Mickey took his place on stage with Sunrise for their opening number. Ronnell, Jalani, Sol, and Medford looked upon him with an encouraging, "You've got this." His mother followed shortly after, taking the mic and giving the crowd a megawatt smile.

During a short break between songs, Lissa blessed the fans with another of her trademark smiles. "Thank you, Twin Cities. Thank you for your warm welcome and thank you for your golden hearts. We of Sunrise appreciate your steadfast support." Brian Bell, seated in the VIP section, shouted his approval. "Thank you, Brian. As always, I want to thank God for the gift He gave me with my voice; Mother, who was there for me from the very beginning; Father, who became my champion; Okeidi, who took a chance on our talent; and my wonderful husband, Michael." The audience cheered. "Tonight, though, is a special night, for two important reasons. It is with great love and pleasure that I introduce the newest addition to Sunrise, my son, Mickey Davis." Mickey stood up, embraced by the waves of love that swept over him in the form of applause.

"And now, I will sing to you my second reason for this night. It is a new song called 'Best Days,' which was written for me by my other son, Allan Arrington-Davis."

Seated between Ramsey and his grandparents, Allan was overwhelmed as he listened to his mother give voice to his melody and lyrics. In his heart, he knew if she sang it, it would be great. The response of the audience confirmed it. Grandma Maureen affectionately squeezed his hand in encouragement. "Proud grandfather" was written all over Grandpa Allan's face. Grandma Saralynne beamed with a full heart. Ramsey's eyes were suspiciously damp. In the middle of the song, Allan had created space for the musicians to showcase their individual talents. When Mickey's time came, Roslyn was swaying in her seat to the rhythm, her face warm as she proclaimed, "That's my man." When the song came to a close, Allan was pleasantly stunned when the audience rose to their feet in a standing ovation.

The concert went like something out of a dream, only made real with the musical contribution of the twins to it, not to mention brotha hugs and back slaps from the Bell branch of the family and "Awww"s from the female relatives. At the curtain call, when Lissa and Michael had Mickey between them, Allan couldn't have been prouder. He could hardly wait to be backstage with hearty congratulations.

The following night saw Allan and Ramsey out on a group date at the bowling alley with Mickey and Roslyn, Hari and Dylan, Ronnell and Lamar, Jermaine and Marcellus, their Bell cousin Brayden, and his boyfriend Trey. At this point, all the couples except Brayden and Trey were married, but Brayden was smart and had put a ring on it.

Their circle was also growing for a different reason. Ronnell and Lamar were fathers to a baby daughter, Erika, and Jermaine and Marcellus were expecting a baby by surrogate. Needless to say, Grandma Bell was over the moon. She loved her grandsons dearly, but the rare arrival of a girl in the family was cause for hosannas and shouting up and down the aisles at church. As for Cousin Wayne and Cousin Theo, they claimed full ownership of the term "doting grandfathers." While Ronnell, Lamar, Jermaine, and Marcellus gushed about fatherhood, Allan was caught up in the thoughts himself. He could have sworn there was a look of longing on Ramsey's face, but it vanished as quickly as it had appeared. Was he imagining things?

Allan luxuriated in his husband's arms, savoring the natural high. Cuddling after mind-blowing lovemaking was always a delicious treat for them. Even in the afterglow, Allan swore he could still feel the delicious pounding Ramsey gave him, and his hole winked. "Mmmmmmm."

"Sounds like my boo is well satisfied." Ramsey gave him a gentle kiss.

"You know it."

"I am beyond happy we met. Maybe it sounds weird, but I knew you were the one."

Allan chuckled. "Not so weird. I remember Cousin Eli and Madear telling me it was love at first sight for them."

"And was it?"

"Bae, when I think back to it, I have to say it was. But the one thing that sealed the deal for me was the day the bridge collapsed. You didn't care about my background or any of that. You were there for me, and you showed how much you cared." *And the vision I had at the lake foresaw it all. He loves me, and he'll never leave me.*

"I wouldn't have been anywhere else, boo."

"You know, I've been thinking a lot lately…about another way we can be there."

"And how's that?"

"With something that would add to our happiness."

"Really? What?"

"Well, it would involve finding a house of our own…with room for our kids."

Ramsey's mouth dropped. "Are you saying…"

"Yeah. I want to start having kids."

"Oh my God. Oh my God. Yeah, boo. I'm ready. I'm so ready for this." Ramsey held Allan even tighter, giving him a long, scuba-diver deep kiss. When they finally surfaced for air, he professed, "I love you, boo. I love you so much."

"I love you too, bae. You're it for me. Now you know, this is something to celebrate. This next phase of our lives."

"Definitely. Tomorrow we go out on the town. But tonight…."

"Yes?"

Ramsey shifted positions so that he was straddling Allan. "Tonight, we go for another round." He ground his ass provocatively against Allan's crotch. "And this time I get to ride your dick like Mister Magic."

Allan's chuckle was low and sexy as he playfully slapped his husband's butt. Ramsey could be such a bossy bottom at times, but he loved it. "Bae, you've got yourself a deal."

Chapter 16

September 2013

Allan and Ramsey knew that the time of their lives was only beginning as their surrogate, Tasha Benson, gave a final push in the delivery room at Sharp Memorial Hospital in San Diego on September 4, 2013. Tasha may have borne a slight resemblance to Janet Jackson, but at that moment, she was a tired and sweaty woman who had endured 10 hours of labor and was ready for it all to be over and done with.

As she groaned through the push, the couple was awestruck as the baby came out and Dr. Marielena Montoya said, "It's a girl." She nodded to Ramsey, who stepped over to cut the umbilical cord. While their daughter was being cleaned up, weighed, and measured, Allan checked on Tasha, who gave him a tired smile, but they knew it wasn't over yet.

11 minutes later, while Ramsey was holding Alana Christine Arrington-Davis, Tasha gave another push and Allan heard Dr. Montoya say, "It's a boy." After he cut the umbilical cord on their son, Daniel Rodney Arrington-Davis, Allan shed more joyous tears with his husband. At last, they were parents!

With each holding a twin, Allan and Ramsey brought them over to see Tasha. They knew Tasha would be a special person in their lives, having given them the most precious, incredible gifts in the world. Already happily married with two children, she was the perfect candidate for them when the search for a suitable match began, thanks to the efforts of family friend and adoption attorney,

Cesare Morelli-Montgomery. Tasha, for her own reasons, only wanted pictures of the babies from time to time, and the young couple well understood and respected the need to protect her privacy.

"How's Tasha doing?" Allan asked Dr. Montoya.

"She's doing fine. Right now, she needs her rest," she replied.

"Not just yet, Doctor. Ramsey, Allan, there's something I'd like us to do first," Tasha said.

Wrapped in almost a group hug, the new parents and the Bensons said a prayer of blessing. After the afterbirths were delivered and she was taken to her hospital suite to spend time with her husband, Allan and Ramsey, still in awe of the tiny bundles in their arms, were taken to the viewing area, where their family and friends eagerly awaited the news. God answered their prayers that the twins were healthy, and with birth weights of five-and-a-half pounds, incubators weren't required.

"Fasten your seat belts, boo, our kids are going to be swept away in love," Ramsey noted as they spotted the waiting crowd gathering on the other side of the window. Holding their daughter up to be seen by everyone, he announced, "Alana, this is your debut."

Allan took his side and propped up their son. "And Daniel, I know you'll do it up fiercely," he said with a laugh.

Allan beamed at Mickey and Roslyn, who were beaming back. Mickey gave his twin a thumbs-up, looking down at his wife's rounded belly and back again with a wink. They too were expecting twins, with Roslyn 15 weeks along. Their respective parents were grinning and making baby faces at them, especially the women. When they first found out that their children were expecting twins, Lissa and Lanita shared an ecstatic, satisfied high-five followed by a "Yes! We *knew* it!!" while Michael and Rodney traded smug grins and fist bumps. Okeidi and Malkia were pleased as Hawaiian Punch, grateful that their efforts to keep everything low-key for the family had paid off, especially when compared to the media frenzy over the birth of William and Kate's son Prince George a mere six weeks ago.

His great-uncles, Uncle Sammy and Uncle Darnell, had a spot up front, sporting celebratory grins. They were in their 90s now, but people would never know it from looking at them because they were still spry and stayed active, even after turning over the operations of their ranch to his Uncle Bernie and Uncle Sherman. And of course, his grandparents were there, with Grandma Saralynne teasing him with exaggerated snoring expressions, Grandpa Allan looking every inch the proud great-grandfather—again, and Grandma Maureen bestowing them with a beatific smile of blessing.

Once they received the green light to take their children home, Allan and Ramsey were on a flight back to the Twin Cities. They were heartily greeted with a welcome-home party at their new home, conveniently located in the Prospect Park area of southeast Minneapolis. Alana and Daniel were passed around like Super Bowl trophies between the women, a glowing, pregnant Roslyn among them.

"Well, we're not gonna to see our kids for a while, probably not until everyone leaves," Ramsey observed.

"Don't fight it, son, enjoy it," Rodney admonished with a little grin. "Look at it this way. You're cultivating your babysitting network. Trust and believe, you're going to need it, especially with twins."

"OK, so we're new at this," Allan added. "Too bad they don't give you road maps for parenthood."

Michael put his arm around Allan's shoulder, ready to impart words of wisdom as Mickey joined the group. "I know, but they don't. Every child is different. It's all on-the-job training. Now, there is one important thing about being a parent that you need to know."

Mickey was all ears as Michael put his other arm around him. "What's that?"

Michael and Rodney trained their eyes on the women—including their wives—who were shamelessly fawning over the twins. "It never stops."

Early in the morning of February 19, 2014, Lissa and Michael, while on a visit to see their grandchildren, received a call from Mickey. "Dad, Roslyn's water broke. We're on our way to the hospital."

"Wait, wait, Mickey," his father said. "Which one?"

"Regions Hospital in St. Paul," was Mickey's nervous reply as they heard a groan on the other end. "She's having a contraction. Gotta go!"

Finding a family member who could look after a pair of five-month-old twins at that hour of the morning was no easy feat but find one they did. Jumping into Allan's Range Rover, Allan, Ramsey, Michael, and Lissa were off to the hospital where they were met by Rodney and Lanita. Nine hours later, Mykel Arrington Davis and Kennedy Roslyn Davis were born 15 minutes apart, weighing in at a respectable five pounds, eleven ounces each.

It was *déjà vu* for Allan as Mickey appeared on the other side of the window to the viewing room, that awestruck, ecstatic expression of joy on his face as he held his new son and daughter in his arms, a tear running down his cheek. He was thrilled for Mickey, finding the love of his life in Roslyn and now being blessed with a double portion. *Thanks God,* he thought as Ramsey's arm wrapped around his waist. Their respective parents were off and running again with baby talk and baby faces, no doubt relishing the fact they had two more grandchildren to spoil.

In the midst of the celebration, the doors to the viewing area opened, and in came his Grandma Saralynne, Grandma Maureen, and Grandpa Allan. After greetings and hugs, Allan asked, "How did you get here so fast?" Remembering his grandfather's access to the company jet, he quickly added, "No, strike that. We're just glad you're here."

"We wouldn't be anywhere else," was his grandfather's heartwarming reply. "How are Alana and Daniel?"

"Well, Alana is the vocal, adventurous one. Danny is more laid-back, but you can't help noticing him. They haven't started crawling yet, but they can turn themselves over. Now, thank God, they sleep through the night. My nights of being a sound sleeper ended the day they came home."

"Sounds like they're coming along just fine," Grandma Saralynne stated. Who's watching them?"

"Cousin Carter and Cousin Julian."

"Well, you know we're not leaving town until after we see them. Now, it's time to see my new great-grands." Grandpa Allan sported a proud, infectious grin.

As the rest of the family was swept up in the euphoria of the moment at the window, Allan stepped back with Ramsey holding him in his arms, and they shared a gentle kiss. Sure, they were tired, snatching sleep where they could when the twins slept and rearranging their schedules. However, it was that good kind of tired. Allan knew they would never be completely out of the eye of the public and the media, but his husband was his ride-or-die guy, and they would handle whatever came along to protect their family.

"Bae, do you remember that slogan, 'It doesn't get any better than this'?" Allan asked.

"Sure, boo. Why?" Ramsey replied with a joyous smile.

"I just got it, bae. I just got it," Allan said warmly as they shared another sweet kiss, followed by a mutual "I love you" before they rejoined the family.

EPILOGUE

June 26, 2015

The air of excitement permeated the crowd waiting outside the Supreme Court building that morning in Washington, D.C. The days had gone by with the various rulings given by the nine justices inside. Yesterday brought happiness to the people gathered there for their beloved president with a favorable ruling on the Affordable Care Act. Today, everyone was waiting and watching.

Allan and Ramsey, Mickey and Roslyn, their respective parents, Sunrise, Uncle Sammy and Uncle Darnell, Grandpa Allan and Grandma Maureen, Grandma Saralynne Davis, and Cousin Eli and Madear were among the contingent of the Christopher family and friends in the expectant crowd surrounding them. It would have been easy to stay home and watch the events unfold on television, but Allan knew that wasn't their way.

He had learned over the years about the power of using his status as a positive, constructive force. Together, he and Ramsey were active in the philanthropic branches of Christopher Electronics and Edwards Enterprises respectively, with the emphatic blessings of Grandpa Allan and Aunt Vickie. With Ramsey by his side and their wonderful children, he had reclaimed himself as part of a family that set standards instead of following them.

"I can only imagine how he's feeling in there right now," Ramsey said.

"If it were me, the suspense would be killing me," Roslyn added.

Allan scanned the crowd for a moment, then back to his family. "All he wanted was to be recognized on his husband's death certificate, that their love was first-class. He wanted the right to be."

"A lot of people have worked long and hard to get to this point." Mickey gave his wife a meaningful look.

"Hey! Check it out," they heard Rodney Arrington call out.

The couples held hands in anticipation when the interns ran from the building, papers in hand, to the area where the news media outlets were stationed. The announcement came. In the next instant, the crowds surrounding them went up in a wave of sustained cheers of elation and tears of joy, the Christopher family right there with them. Marriage equality was now the law of the land.

Allan was beside himself. He couldn't stop grinning. Balloons were released into the sky. Signs waved enthusiastically with messages of "Love wins" and "Love won out." Amidst all the hugs and celebration in the family, he and Ramsey made their way over to Uncle Sammy and Uncle Darnell. They were wrapped up in an embrace, tears streaming down their faces after they shared a kiss.

"We made it. We actually lived to see this day," Darnell beamed, wiping his eyes as more hugs were exchanged.

"We certainly have," was Sammy's heartfelt sentiment. "There's going to be some major celebrating at the ranch tonight."

Just then Eli and Madear joined them, sharing the love. Eli had an aura of gratitude and satisfaction about him, knowing that one of his visions had brought so much happiness to so many who had been long denied. The family knew that sooner or later, reporters would come nosing around for a sound bite, and they weren't disappointed. However, they would, as they always had, protect Eli and his "gift," as well as his descendants who inherited it.

Along with Grandpa Allan, Vickie, Tanya, Lissa, and Michael fielded the questions from the press while lawn chairs were provided for the older relatives to rest. During the interviews, Lissa's mind went back to the moment nine years ago when Eli revealed his vision, leaving her with a sense of awe. Returning to the present, she heard her husband respond to a question from the reporter and motioned for her sons and their spouses to join them.

"About 30 years ago, my brother-in-law, my nephews, and my niece wanted to bring the persons of their choice to their senior prom, and those persons happened to be of the same sex," Michael said. "In support of them, Sunrise wrote a song called 'The Right to Be.'" He turned to his sons. "That song is as relevant now as it was then, probably more so on this day. Today, this decision says that Allan and Ramsey's love is as valid and equal as Mickey and Roslyn's. We wouldn't have it any other way."

"I didn't support my son or my grandchildren back then. I was one of those men who didn't want to rock the boat," Grandpa Allan said, his eyes now watery. "Things changed in my heart when I realized how I was hurting them. They were far braver than I was. This day means so much, not only to my family, but to countless families here and around the U.S. I'm not saying that we won't have any more hurdles, but this is no longer one of them. And as for the Christopher family—I know you're all out there watching—let me say I love you and how proud I am of all of you."

"Thank you for sharing that, Mr. Christopher." The reporter turned to Allan. "And what does this day mean for you?"

The twins faced each other and shared a laugh. "Well, since we have kids, we're going to go celebrate with them," Allan replied. "I know a lot of people are going to say this, and probably already have, but a day will come down the road when Alana and Danny and Mykel and Kennedy will look back at this time and wonder what all the fuss was about. In the meantime, we're going to enjoy this day for all it's worth."

"That's right. Today is all about sharing the love," Mickey concurred.

Later, in their hotel suite, Allan and Ramsey watched President Obama's speech honoring the decision via YouTube while Alana and Danny curled up beside them, moved by his words. Dylan and Hari Langley-Spencer, now the doting parents of a daughter, had called earlier in celebration of the game-changing news. Grandpa Allan already confirmed their presence for the Christopher family victory party to be held that evening in one of the ballrooms. Okeidi had called Lissa and Michael earlier, thrilled with the news while she eagerly filled them in about the requests pouring in for "The Right to Be" since the news broadcast. Not only that, DJs in Chicago were playing it in response to the Supreme Court decision.

"You think Uncle Bernie's checking this out?" Ramsey asked.

Allan gave his husband a mock incredulous look. "Do you even have to ask? They were trailblazers in their own right back in the day at Evanston East High. Him, Diane, Mac, and Val. I'm sure once Mom tells him what the DJs in Chicago are doing, he'll stay over the moon."

"Not to mention his family."

"There you go." A playful smirk graced Allan's face as he thought of Uncle Bernie and Uncle Sherman's sons—Jesse with his boyfriend Durrell, Bruce and his boyfriend Jorge, and Sam's comments about the cute guys in his high school. Noting the curious look on Ramsey's face, he became conspiratorial. "Before we came out here, Jesse told me something."

"Like what?"

"He said if the Supreme Court greenlighted marriage equality, he was going to propose to Durrell today."

"No way!"

"Way."

"Like Cousin Wayne says, 'Honey hush. Let me be the fly on the wall for that one.'" To accommodate the sleeping form of Danny beside him, Ramsey shifted to a more comfortable position next to Allan on the bed. "I hope he makes a video of it. But hey. It's all about love today, and love is victorious. Just like it was the day I met you, boo."

Allan took time to beam at Alana, sound asleep in his lap, then Danny, and finally a deep gaze into the eyes of the man he loved, saying those three magic words with his "Beckley eyes" before he went in for a kiss.

ABOUT THE AUTHOR

W.D. Foster-Graham is a native son of Minneapolis, Minnesota. He received a B.A. in psychology from Luther College, with a minor in Black studies. He is an original member of the 3-time Grammy Award-winning ensemble, Sounds of Blackness. He has also been recognized by the International Society of Poets as one of its "Best New Poets of 2003," and is a guest writer for Wyatt O'Brian Evans (The Huffington Post, the Washington Post, the Advocate). He is the book review editor for Insight News, a Black community newspaper in the Twin Cities.

A 5-time published author, his passion for writing was inspired by his father, who read voraciously. His tastes in writing run to historical fiction, family sagas, and romance, seasoned with his own brand of African American flavor—at the end of the day, it's all about the love. He shamelessly admits to a love of romance novels, whodunits, and classic movies of old Hollywood. He also received inspiration from the late novelists E. Lynn Harris and Toni Morrison. In Toni's words, "If there is a story you wish to read, and it hasn't been written yet, then you must be the one to write it."

Retired from the field of teaching, he loves travel on the open road and time with his husband and son when not in writer's mode.

Made in the USA
Monee, IL
27 October 2021

80932657R00094